Left

Left

A Love Story

Mary Hogan

An Imprint of HarperCollinsPublishers

HarperCollins books may be purchased for educational, business, or sales promotional use. For information please e-mail the Special Markets Department at SPsales@harpercollins.com.

FIRST HARPERLUXE EDITION

ISBN: 978-0-06-284580-1

HarperLuxe™ is a trademark of HarperCollins Publishers.

Library of Congress Cataloging-in-Publication Data is available upon request.

18 19 20 21 22   ID/LSC   10 9 8 7 6 5 4 3 2 1

To my dad
Edward Arthur Barbera
1924–2012

"The past beats inside me like a second heart."
JOHN BANVILLE, *THE SEA*

Chapter One

I never meant for it to happen. Though, isn't that what they all say? My heart was at the wheel; my mind and body were buckled, helpless, in the backseat? Lola was along for the ride, of course. Best friends like her appear only once or twice or maybe three times in a lifetime.

Lola—leggy, striking, indifferent—was standing a few feet back when love broadsided me. More precisely, when lust hit in a T-bone collision. Because that's what it was. Blind and combustible *want*. A longing so fiery I felt like a flushed teenager. As if I would incinerate if we didn't connect.

"Lola. Look."

She didn't look. She hated to be told what to do. Silently, I pulled her closer. You were surrounded by red geraniums, lit by summer's lemon macaron of a sun.

Brazenly, I lifted my chin to take in your full height. Tall, stately, a touch of gray. Never had I seen such a flawless exterior, so utterly smooth. I longed to reach my hand up, touch, stroke gently with the backs of my fingers. My eyelids quivered. Lola couldn't bear to look at my foolishness.

I stepped forward; Lola stepped back. We both paused at the base of your granite steps, scrubbed and sparkling. The two of us squinted in the gleam bouncing off your front door. Your glass sat behind a swirl of wrought iron, within a rectangle of shiny black trim. The fluid finish was clearly the work of an ox-hair brush. And, of course, a superior undercoat. Probably Hollandlac. Worth every dollar. Bookending your regal entrance were two holly shrubs, shaped to conical perfection. Above them, copper light fixtures with the dusty gray of a natural patina. Peaked bulbs resembled a gaslight's dancing flames.

"I'm going in." My legs lifted me up the steps. Lola hung back. The leather strap in my hand slipped through my fingers. I reached for your brass grip—rub-polished with a chamois, not a cloth, to a depth of gold that stole my breath. Inside, I saw a marble vestibule. Mosaic edging. Beyond it—was that stained glass?

"May I help you?"

From within your vast lobby, a doorman appeared. His uniform was sedate: black slacks and bow tie, short-sleeved white shirt. No stiff suit with brass buttons or epaulets. No white gloves or pilot hat. Understated class. Like you. He was in his late thirties, early forties, maybe. Cocky in a sexy sort of way. He opened the door and blocked my entrance.

"I, um, well, see—" What exactly could I say? I'd been walking down the street, teetering on the brink of despair, when *blam*, I fell in love with his building? Its perfection tugged me up the stairs as if I were in a trance? My heart knew that nothing bad could happen to me beyond its guarded doors. Inside, I would be forever safe.

I blinked at him. He stared at me. Silently, I debated ways to explain my desire without sounding demented. Could I confess that, lately, I felt like I was living in the middle of an icy lake? Cracks everywhere. Frozen in panic. At any moment, I could be plunged into its frigid depths? Was managing emotional terror part of a doorman's purview? Or was he primarily there for the dry-cleaning delivery?

"Your dog, ma'am." The doorman flicked his head.

I wheeled around. Lola had followed her nose into the middle of the street.

"Come!" I yelled.

She didn't come. Of course not. She never came when I called, only when I didn't want her underfoot, like when I was searching the floor for a dropped Xanax.

Thankfully, we were on Hudson Crescent, a curved sliver of leafy street tucked into a nook between Riverside Drive and West End Avenue. A patch of green separated the Crescent from the Drive, so Lola wasn't in danger of being flattened by a bus or a speeding cab. Hardly anyone even walked on the Crescent. Which was why I'd taken this route into the park. So I could hide. So I could cry behind my sunglasses.

Nonetheless, I flew down the steps into the street to grab Lola's leather leash. She had no car savvy. None. If a car did decide to loop off the Drive and onto the Crescent, Lola would stare at it with her stoner eyes, annoyed by the rubbery smell of its tires.

With Lola's leash firmly in hand, I pulled her onto the sidewalk. Stupidly, I said, "Good girl," even though she'd been bad. The doorman had stepped outside. I didn't want him to think I was one of those emotional wrecks who spank a child or a dog out of fear.

"Heel," I added, yanking Lola in line.

Standing like a sentry on your top granite step, the doorman crossed his arms over his chest. His body language said, "Move along, missy." I opened my mouth to protest, to tell him I only *looked* like a dog walker with my dusty sneakers and saggy denim shorts. But, suddenly, I saw myself as he saw me: a middle-aged woman with love handles. A buyer of clothes from Target, because, well, why not? A person with no business in his building. What had I been thinking? A building like you would never go for a woman in my current state. Silently, I cursed myself for not wearing lipstick. For not brushing my hair or maybe even my teeth that morning. How had I let things unravel so?

With a lovesick sigh, I flapped a melancholy wave and moved along. Lola squirted a spritz of pee onto the base of your ornate streetlight, telling him, in her own way, that we would be back.

"Good girl," I muttered under my breath.

We walked through the Crescent to the path in the green that led to the Drive. There, we waited for the light before crossing the street into Riverside Park. As we ventured deeper into the trees, I felt our connection tug at my back. Was that stained glass beyond your lobby? Had I seen a brass *railing*? Did front apartments have a mind-blowing view of the river?

Once more, I felt the exhilaration of desire.

Lola pressed her nose into a clump of ryegrass and inhaled. I sighed. After it was all over, maybe we could live in that pristine place? With a doorman in a bow tie to keep unpleasantness outside your wrought-iron door, I'd forget the heartache of our trip to Spain, the incident that had started the downhill tumble. I'd forgive myself for looking away when so many signs were in front of my face. My messy life would be tidy again.

By the end of our walk that day, I was sure. Determined, even. Eleven Eighteen Hudson Crescent was where Lola and I would relocate. After. So I could remember the inferno of love.

Chapter Two

It's true what they say about light in Spain. It's unlike any other. Especially late in the day, when a persimmon sun begins to melt. Paul and I watched the colors of Málaga change from pink to purple to red on the patio of our rented cottage. We drank glasses of cherry-colored wine straight from the barrels of Casa de Guardia. Fresh figs—plucked from a tree at the foot of the mountain—lodged their seeds in our teeth; wedges of Idiazabal cheese released a smoky aroma into the air.

"We should live like this at home," I said, languidly. "*Tapas y vino.*"

"And siestas." Paul suggestively bobbed his abundant eyebrows up and down. He stretched his palm out; I rested my hand on top of it and squeezed. After all these years, I liked that my husband still wanted to make love in the afternoon. Tilting my head in a seductive way, I said, "In your chambers? On your desk?" Two weeks of Spanish bliss were his gift to me. The least I could do was return the favor.

Paul erupted in the laugh I fell in love with. Deep and unapologetic. "*¿Por qué no?*"

Why not, indeed?

All summer, back home in Manhattan, Paul's ex had been popping over unannounced. "Fay!" she'd chirp into our intercom. Only she made it a two-syllable word: Fay-*ee*. It irked me to no end. Nearly as grating as the name my parents gave me at birth: Faith. What were they thinking? Combined with my original last name, Thayer, it's impossible to say both without sounding like you have a lisp. Faith Thayer. *Thee?* The moment I left home for college, I abbreviated it to "Fay" and have never looked back. Besides, "Faith" sounds so *Sister Wives.* As if I live with Hope and Charity in a sprawling Utah colonial, counting the days until it's my turn to peel back the covers and invite my polygamist husband into bed.

"Fay-*ee!*"

"Who's this?" I knew. Of course. Our duplex in an old New York brownstone has only a front-door buzzer. No video intercom, no doorman to keep the riffraff out.

All I can do is press the audio button and say, "Yes?" whenever the buzzer ignites Lola's barking frenzy. The way it did the week before we left for Spain.

"Is Paul home?" Brenda, no dummy, knew I recognized her voice.

Bark, bark.

"He's in court. As he is every day."

"I've come all the way from Jersey."

"Still. Not home."

I was working. Paint was drying.

"Mind if I come in for a minute?"

Bark, bark.

"Shut it!"

"*Excuse* me?" Brenda's mood often turned on a dime.

"Lola is going berserk."

Contrary to her volume when the front door buzzes, Lola isn't a beagle or a mini schnauzer or a Westie. She's a large hound blend from a kill shelter in Arkansas. The seedy circumstances of her conception—a rushed encounter behind a gas station Dumpster, I heard—nonetheless produced a uniquely stunning girl. Her short white coat is speckled with black; her silver flop-over ears are as soft as rabbit fur. People who don't know dogs—and kids—think she's a Dalmatian.

"She has freckles, not spots." I smile to camouflage

my displeasure whenever my genius girl is mistaken for one of those numbskulls from the Disney movie.

Paul and I have been unable to stop Lola's buzzer barking for her entire eight-year life. Protecting her turf is hardwired into her DNA. As is her feline demeanor. When she's not barking at the door, Lola is as haughty as a Russian Blue. She's always been more cat than dog.

"Have you tried a shock collar?" Brenda asked through the intercom.

I buzzed her in. As I always did. What else could I do?

Brenda's latest reason for dropping by from her home in Ridgewood, New Jersey—a full twenty miles away—was to announce that she had reinvented herself as a meditation coach. Whatever the hell that was. "How nice for you," I said, not offering a chair or even a glass of water.

"I was wondering . . ."

I stifled an eye roll. Those were the three words Brenda Agarra used most around me and my husband.

"I was wondering, Paul, if you might consider upping my alimony."

"I was wondering if you knew anyone who's interested in buying a used mattress?"

Honestly, I wondered how my husband could ever have married such a flake. "Youth." That's all Paul had to say about that. He was too much of a gentleman to bad-mouth the mother of his son. He was also too generous to curtail Brenda's intrusion in our lives. I'd be happy if she was barred from the city entirely. Some roadblock, maybe, on the George Washington Bridge? I mean, the woman has a whole *house* in New Jersey. She thinks I should electrocute my dog. Still, I put up and shut up for the sake of a happy family. Bad blood between an ex and a current never does anyone any good. Too many scheduling conflicts at Thanksgiving.

"I was wondering," Brenda said that day, "if Paul would consider a personal loan so I can build a meditation studio behind the house."

Again, I quashed the urge to roll my eyes.

"What kind of repayment schedule are we talking here, Brenda?"

"Hm. I'll have to meditate on that."

When Paul got home that night, we both had a hearty laugh.

My husband was right. As judges tend to be. A vacation in Spain was exactly what I needed. Bare feet on warm Saltillo tile. Time in slo-mo. Dinner at ten. Wine at five. Siestas. Lazy afternoons making love. Me and my man. Life as it should be.

"To us," Paul said, raising his glass into the auburn light.

Chapter Three

It shouldn't have worked. Paul Agarra, a sitting New York State Supreme Court criminal judge, was forty-five when we met; I was twenty-four. Recently graduated from art school, I did what most art school grads did: I worked as a waitress. It was one of those dark pubs in lower Manhattan that smelled like grooming cream and business suits that were regularly saturated in flop sweat. First-year law associates met there to gripe about the partners in their firms. Female attorneys drank scotch there. Male lawyers sat at the bar, shouting and shoving greasy peanuts into their faces.

"What can I get you?" I set a square white napkin in front of Paul. He had tan hands and gray sideburns. Gingerbread-colored eyes. He sat alone at a small table near the back.

"Earplugs?"

I laughed. It was always loud in there. "Two pearl onions? A couple of olives?"

"Only if they come with a martini."

"Gin or vodka?"

"Vodka."

"Dry, perfect, or wet?"

"Yes."

I laughed again. It was clear he was flirting, yet he was terrible at it. He even blushed. I liked him right away.

"Are you a lawyer?" Silently, I prayed *no*. The lawyers I'd met were boorish, boring, or so obsessed with making partner they had hunchbacks from lugging case files around. Plus, few tipped more than 10 percent. Even the partners.

"Worse," Paul whispered. "I'm a judge. Don't blow my cover."

"Your secret is safe with me."

After that initial meeting, Paul came in for a drink once or twice a week. We got to know each other in two-minute spurts. He had a prickly teenage son; I had a troubled family in California. He was funny; I was serious about finding a way to make a living as an artist. He lived in a modern two-bedroom in Battery Park that he hated; I lived with my best friend, Anita—whom I adored—in Brooklyn. Months later, when Paul asked me out, he blushed again when he said, "You can say no if you want to."

"Why would I want to say no?"

"I'm forty-five."

My lips curved into a grin. "Good thing I'm old enough to say yes."

Later, I found out that Judge Paul Agarra first came into the pub where I worked because he'd seen me through the window.

"Sometimes you just *know*," he said.

He was right, as judges tend to be.

"Will you be my love for life?" On one knee—truly—that's how Paul proposed. I opened my heart and invited him in. I knew, too.

My brilliant judge. We got married on a Sunday morning in his courtroom. Paul's law clerk, Isaac Lewis, officiated. He got ordained for the specific purpose of marrying us, which felt exactly right. Paul and Isaac spent more waking hours together than Paul and I did. Isaac was Paul's work wife, though he hated it when I said that. A former marine, he could still bench-press 220.

I remember that day in snapshots. Oak pews the color of Meyer lemons, marble floors as shiny as windows. Isaac stood as tall as a Viking behind Paul's desk. He wore a dark blue suit and a white tie. As did Paul. I wore a lacy dress and held a small bouquet of red roses. Two wisteria garlands decorated the central aisle. My brothers, Nathan and Joey, had flown in from California. Anita was my maid of honor. Paul's son, John, was his best man. Brenda wasn't invited.

"She had her wedding day," I'd decreed. "This one is mine."

Brenda would have shown up in a long, flowing white dress. Of that, I had no doubt. Probably flowers in her hair, too.

On that clear Sunday morning—a postcard of a New York day—my dad wept as he walked me down the aisle to the man I would promise myself to for life. Friends seated in the courtroom pews pressed their hands to their chests and said, "Aw." When Dad didn't stop, they moved their hands up to their mouths so they could whisper behind them. Quietly, Nathan led him out a side door. After Mom died, Dad never could control his emotions.

Whenever I think back on that day, I mostly smile. Sometimes, my heart breaks, too. Nathan had said, "Mom is here in spirit." But I so wanted her there in the flesh. I longed to burrow into her hug and feel the warmth of her breath on my ear as she whispered, "He's everything I ever wanted for you."

Mom would have adored Paul. She would have loved

our wedding. It was a reflection of my new husband and me: atypical, but perfectly *us*. We hosted the small reception around a large table at our favorite restaurant in Chinatown. Our white cake from Magnolia Bakery was layered with banana pudding.

True love in every way.

Chapter Four

I'd pushed for sightseeing. Of course. Málaga—the birthplace of Picasso—is an artist's dream. Color everywhere. The Persian blue Mediterranean Sea, butter yellow high-rises, marmalade rooftops, basil green mountains, air the color of honey. Paul would have been happy relaxing at the cottage, puzzling over words like "spork" in the *New York Times* crossword. Not me. I needed to see color the way other women needed to eat chocolate.

"Orange." It's what John—Paul's teenage son—had answered when I'd asked him what color he wanted to paint his bedroom.

"Carrot, pumpkin, or cantaloupe?" My face was as inscrutable as Mona Lisa's. Back then, John was in a *Trainspotting* phase. Peroxided hair, black turtlenecks,

Lou Reed, heroin chic. He liked to test us. In those early days, I was a young stepmother learning on the fly.

Stupidly, Paul and I bought a run-down duplex apartment on Manhattan's Upper West Side when we were newlyweds. Marriage, I learned quickly, was hard enough without Sheetrock dust all over your clothes. Still, the moment I set foot in that space, I knew it was my home. Two bedrooms, two bathrooms, a bricked garden on the ground floor. And, its own special gift: a sunny nook for my easel. It was everything I ever wanted. Worth our sweat and tears.

Every other weekend, Paul's son lived with us. When it came time to paint his room, he smirked when he replied, "Carrot."

Paul weighed in from behind a newspaper. "N.O."

"It's my room!" All teenage grimace and pimply flush, John stamped his foot like a child.

"In my apartment," said Paul.

"*Our* apartment," I gently reminded him. "And it's John's room. Why not let him pick the color? It's only paint."

Paul shot me a dark look; I helped him lighten up.

In the paint store, John chose a sickening nacho color. Paul opened his mouth to protest, but I silenced him with a tented brow. What did it matter? John was a good kid. A teenager, yes—moody, slouchy, occasionally reeking of hormonal funk—but tolerable. He chuckled when I said, "We should get two dogs named George and Ringo. You know, round out the band?" I loved him for not groaning. When John was with his dad, Paul, I'm sure he heard comments like that all the time.

Seriously, I could have done worse. Paul could have had a daughter.

"It's not like he's *doing* heroin," I quietly told my brand-new husband.

In the screech of a Primal Scream CD, the three of us painted the walls—and ceiling!—of John's bedroom. Afterward, sitting on the floor eating pizza, Paul's son looked around and said, "This is the ugliest room I've ever seen."

We all got a good laugh out of that.

John is a coder now. He lives in Boston with a beautiful wife and amazing daughter. Like I said, it was only paint.

"Fay is wise beyond my years." It's Paul's favorite quip. Or was. Whenever he said it, he threw his head back and howled at his own cleverness. My husband's laugh was an invitation to join his party. What I wouldn't give to hear that sound one more time.

———

"**Grilled sardines** on the beach in El Palo?" I suggested on our cottage patio, in Spain's afternoon light.

"Too many Speedos."

"A trek up Gibralfaro?"

"So darn uphill."

"How about a stroll along Calle Larios in central Málaga?"

"Watch every Latin lover ogle my wife?"

"Paul."

"Spoon and fork!" he yelped, filling in the crossword. Then he set the puzzle aside and joined me in touring Málaga. Because he loved me.

I loved that city. It felt like warm bread to me. Irresistible. The sort of city a person could devour when she felt cold or empty.

Each day, Paul and I strolled the *avenidas*. Leisurely, like Spaniards. We left our New York pace at home. In the nave of La Manquita, we blessed ourselves with holy water and sat in dark pews to soak up the angelic rays slanting down from the heavenly stained glass windows. My husband lassoed me into the crook of his arm, pressed a kiss on my temple, and whispered, "Seeing you in this light is worth the trip."

I grinned, blissful. Wrapping my arm around Paul's soft waist, I quietly leaned in to kiss the baby skin under his chin, the spot I owned. My body fit so snugly into his I almost heard a *click* as we interlocked. In Paul Agarra's devouring hug, the world and its perils were safely caged away.

Our life is a postcard, I thought, clueless. With a contented smile, I rested my cheek against my husband's strong shoulder.

Love as it should be.

Not once, not ever, did I regret my choice. Not after our first anniversary or our last one: our twenty-second. In the early days of our marriage, I raised my right hand in the air and vowed, "I, Fay Agarra, do solemnly swear to allow my husband to be exactly who he is." Paul promised, too. Our word to each other. We'd never expect the other to be older or younger. Paul wasn't my dad; I wasn't his midlife crisis. In the shower, Paul sang obscure blues songs about somebody doing somebody wrong. I danced the Macarena in our living room. I added blond streaks to the front of my brown hair; Paul let his temples go peppery gray. I tolerated his Tom Selleck mustache (for a while); he patiently waited for me to blow-dry my "Rachel."

After two miscarriages, my husband consoled an inconsolable me. He softly said, "Okay, love," when I refused to try again. After my mother, my brother, my dad, I couldn't bear to lose anyone else.

Men my age seemed like boys, heads bent over their cell phones as if the present moment was never riveting enough. Eyes roaming the other tables in a restaurant; brows cocked when a woman asked a waiter, "Do fries come with that?"

Paul is different. He's a grown man. Words of commitment never get trapped behind overly bleached teeth.

I love you. You're mine. We're us.

Yeah, it shouldn't have worked. Yet it did. Until it didn't.

Chapter Five

I awoke to the smell of warm *bollos* and hot *cortados*. Spain's version of coffee and rolls. Paul was just back from the village. Propping myself up in bed, I announced, "I must see the Alcazaba in the Alhambra."

"Where Colonel Mustard waits for Miss Scarlet with a candlestick?"

"Ha-ha." In my pajama tee, I slapped my bare feet over to the kitchen table and pulled my coffee out of the bag. The simplicity of our cottage soothed me. The white walls were textured, the dark beams were rough. A thin cotton bedspread—a mind-blowing electric blue—showed every wrinkle in the sheets.

It was perfect. But I wanted above and beyond. Of course. Had I not always reached for more, more, more, never satisfied with the status quo, what happened would not have happened. I could have lived on in blissful ignorance. For a while, at least.

"Seriously, Paul," I said, "this is a must-see situation."

"Please tell me it's not another uphill trek."

"Not exactly."

He narrowed his eyes at me. I said, "It's in Granada."

"What? Have you forgotten that we leave tomorrow?"

After a swig of creamed espresso, I said, "I have it all figured out. We'll take a commuter flight tomorrow morning, see the Alcazaba and the Alhambra, take a thousand photos, then fly back to the Málaga airport in plenty of time to catch our flight home."

"Fay."

"It's *the* Alcazaba in *the* Alhambra. When else are we going to see a medieval Islamic palace?"

Paul bit into a roll. "Didn't we see the Alibaba *here*?"

"Yes, there's an *Alcazaba* in Málaga. Which is how I remembered the other one. The famous one. I need to go. It's for work."

He groaned. When I played the work card, it was hard to say no. Finally, I was making money. Thank you, Etsy! My small business, Made on the Shade, had taken off. I had a backlog of orders. I'd swapped my easel and fantasy of a star-studded gallery opening for a flat drafting table, blank canvas lampshades, and a (modest) living. My bulletin board at home was littered with inspirational photos.

Crime scene photos were Paul's art. He'd seen every unimaginable way a person can deface a human body. In his courtroom, from his perch on the bench, he'd studied the vacant gazes of murderers, rapists, pedophiles, robbers who terrorized their victims with shaking gun barrels pressed to their temples. He'd searched for humanity.

"I'm ashamed. I have a mother. I can't imagine any-one being evil enough to do this to her. The night I killed your son, I was blinded by a rage I couldn't control. I will use my time in prison to search my soul for the answer you need most: Why? That's my promise to you."

That's what a grieving mother needed to hear. At the very least.

"On the night it happened," a typical allocution began. As if a bolt of lightning did the killing. As if the defendant wasn't even in the room or on the block. "I was high on meth (ox, vico, black tar, China white) and don't remember anything."

Authentic remorse was as rare as a surgeon apolo-gizing for a nicked aorta. "Closure." A ridiculous word some journalist made up. When Paul came home to me, he fell into my arms to forget. He loved the color I brought into our lives; I loved the stability. And *him*. Paul Agarra was the sort of man who surprised his wife with a cottage vacation in Spain when life pressed too heavily down on her head.

"If I want repeat orders," I'd said that morning in Málaga, "I need to expand my line. You know that. I'm thinking Nasrid borders."

Paul rolled his neck in a complete circle. "Will we have to rent a car?"

"Already booked it."

Chapter Six

The fire hydrant sat in the shade of a ginkgo tree around the corner from 1118 Hudson Crescent. I looped Lola's long leash around it, leaving enough slack for her to sniff every millimeter of the hydrant without reaching the tree bed. Then I tickled the tussock of hair atop her head and said, "I won't be long." She didn't whine or tug at the leash. She was happy to be left alone. At last, she had the chance to give a New York City fire hydrant the olfactory exploration it deserved. Pee mails from every dog in the neighborhood.

With a sucked-in stomach, I straightened my shirt. I was ready. My Spanx jeans held everything in place. A Brooks Brothers tailored blouse—arctic white, professionally pressed, cuffs rolled to mid-forearms— was suitably patrician. As were my new periwinkle mesh sneakers from J.Crew. Most importantly, my hair looked perfect. Thanks to Anita. The day before, she had dropped by the apartment. When she saw me, she shook her head and announced, "Fay, you look like a Yeti." Admittedly, it was true. Once my life began to slip, my look did, too.

Opening her leather bag, Anita plunged her hand into its depths. She fished around until her fingers landed on the familiar rectangle of her phone. Her thumb was already in position when she retrieved her cell. I watched her expertly scroll down her contacts list and tap a name. "Can you squeeze a friend in for an emergency intervention?"

I grinned. Sometimes I wanted to fling my arms around Anita Pritchard and hold on forever.

With my fresh cut and color, and classic outfit, I made my way to your granite steps. It was time to take our relationship to the next level. I mussed my shiny brown hair. Looking too coiffed would look desperate. I wanted a breezy appearance. As if I'd taken a morning sail in the Hamptons before dashing for the Jitney.

"Good morning." Your doorman was different from the man I'd seen before. Younger. More darkly handsome. With a serene expression, I said, "I'm considering apartments in this neighborhood. Thought I'd check you out." Then I tacked on a lie: "I'm moving to the city from Silicon Valley."

Chad—the name I gave him for his broody soap opera looks—turned and walked to a podium in your breathtaking lobby. It sat in the spill of light from a modern chandelier: a glowing mass of crystal gum balls. I followed Chad inside. "Nice," I said, nonchalantly.

"Here." He held out a business card. "This broker handles our sales."

My cheeks flushed with pleasure. He assumed I was a *buyer*, not a renter. As I'd hoped, my outfit spoke of summers on Shelter Island, winters in St. Barts. Delicately, I plucked the card from Chad's tan hands and pretended to read it without my glasses.

"I'll give them a buzz," I said. "I'm Fay, by the way. Fay Agarra." I injected a touch of emphasis into my married name. As if he should know it. It landed perfectly. Chad's abundant eyebrows lifted. His dark eyes momentarily flashed white. He said, "I'm Juan Carlos."

My heart trilled. Better than Chad. Not Juan. Not Carlos. *Juan Carlos.* How incredibly inclusive.

"Mind if I look around the lobby, Juan Carlos?" I asked, sweetly. Fleetingly, I wondered if I would call him J.C. after I moved in.

"Sorry, ma'am."

"Thank yo—*pardon?*"

"Our real estate agent will show you around. With an appointment."

To tour the *lobby*? It took a moment to regain my equilibrium. I brushed my hair back to reveal the diamond studs Paul had given me on our fifteenth anniversary. "I went rogue," he'd said, handing me the velvet box. "Officially, it should be rubies." Oh, how we'd laughed back then.

Juan Carlos didn't move. Neither did I. Though I did tilt my head slightly to make sure my earrings caught the chandelier's light.

Just then, an elderly resident entered your vestibule. A Pomeranian panted at her heels. He had the face of a vampire bat. Juan Carlos hurried to hold open your door.

"Some idiot leashed their dog to the hydrant outside," the woman snarled. "The abandoned dog is just sitting there looking forlorn."

Accidentally, I guffawed. After years as Lola's mom, I knew every one of her facial expressions: jaded, arrogant, indifferent, hungry, expectant, and her specialty—the heavy-lidded bleary stare of a teenager who sneaks hits of weed in the bathroom. Never would she lower herself to look forlorn.

Quickly, I covered my guffaw with a gasp. "A fire hydrant? In the glaring sun?"

"Well, no," she said. "It's in the shade. Still."

"Still," I repeated, shaking my head in commiseration. "I'm going to call the ASPCA this minute. I, too, am a dog lover. Juan Carlos, I'll be over there. On that antique bench."

Without waiting for a response, I strode into the belly of your massive lobby with the bearing of Queen Elizabeth. The first one. Curling my lips over my teeth, I bit down on a squeal of delight.

"*Aarah, aarah.*"

The batty dog filled the air with his shrill yips. He didn't have the lung power to summon a proper bark. His frothy caramel-colored coat looked like a vat of cotton candy. His tail curled over his back. At least I thought he was male. Who could tell with all that fluff?

"*Aarah, aarah, aarah.*"

"Benny, hush," said the old woman.

Male. Good thing. Lola was often a bitch around girls.

"Ma'am—" Juan Carlos made an effort to oust me, but I cut him off.

"One minute. Two tops." Now that I was inside you, there would be no easily getting me out. I sat on the polished butler's bench in your alcove. I pulled my iPhone out of my pocket and silently prayed no one would notice it was three generations old. With my back Pilates straight, I pretended to Google the ASPCA.

"You're a dear." The old woman and her mutt climbed your three stairs—marble! polished brass railings!—leading to a far wing of your massive lobby. I longed to follow her and feel your cool embrace as you swallowed me up. Instead, I smiled like a cult member. I gave the elderly resident sufficient time to memorize my face in case she was on the co-op board. By the time they interviewed me, she would have forgotten about the dog at the hydrant. If not, I'd tell her Lola was a service dog. Her temporary attachment to the fire hydrant was training, I'd say. I'd been timing it on my phone. If necessary, I'd buy Lola a yellow vest online. She hates yellow. And vests. Still.

"I'm on hold," I called over to Juan Carlos, waggling my phone in the air. He nodded and returned to his post. In the glow of the interior stained glass windows— lit from behind—I sat back against the spindles of your antique bench. The textured glass scene: a winding, flower-edged path, a thatched-roof cottage, and a blue sky cast a rainbow pattern on my white blouse. I released a soft sigh as I looked around your spotless lobby. No doubt about it. Here, shielded from the untidy world, a middle-aged woman with a broken heart could start over.

Chapter Seven

It wasn't possible. Granada was more gorgeous than Málaga. Madison Avenue meets the village square. Sunlight sparked off storefront windows. Limestone facades were scrubbed to the color of bread flesh. Above the street, in terraced apartments, hanging begonias spilled over black wrought-iron railings. Pink, peach, red. Leaves as green as zucchini skin. Gauzy white curtains billowed in the breeze.

"So, where's this place?"

Paul looked uneasy. The highway from the airport was smooth and wide. "Like driving on velvet," he said. But central Granada was a maze of narrow cobblestoned streets. Motorcycles leaned on the edges of their tires as they knitted in and out of traffic. Pedestrians disobeyed crosswalk lines. Paul's eyes darted around like a pinball. He held the steering wheel in a death grip.

"Follow the signs up the hill," I said.

In our rental car, Paul nervously lurched up a steep hill, through a high-end neighborhood, around a traffic loop. Jade spindles of skinny cypress trees jabbed the air. White stucco estates sat squat beneath their red-tile roofs. The sky was ridiculously blue. I took pictures out the window and stared at everything long enough to burn it into my brain. When I got home, I would mix Perylene maroon with Naples yellow and add a dot of titanium. Maybe the softest dab of cadmium orange? I would work until I got that Spanish roof color just right.

"Park there," I said, pointing. The lot was at the top of the hill, but at the bottom of a mountain.

"We can't drive up?"

"The Alhambra was built in the ninth century, Paul. Like, a thousand years before cars."

With a sigh, he parked. Together, we got out of the car and looked up. At the same time I said, "Wow," Paul said, "Whew." He seemed relieved to have made it.

"Am I right?" I asked. "A must-see?"

Rising into the sky like a pile of glowing Christmas gifts were thirty rectangular towers of various heights. The Alhambra—the palace of Muslim kings—and the stone fortress of the Alcazaba within it, occupied the entire mountaintop. Its celestial color—a shade between pink and orange—was a stunning reflection of Spain's luminescence. Light unlike any other.

Out of the corner of my eye, I saw Paul rub his knees.

"You okay?" I asked.

He nodded. Then he said, "Mind if I sit this one out?"

"What? Why?"

"My sixty-seven-year-old body is saying hello."

I swallowed a groan and arranged my features into a compassionate look. "Want me to stay with you?" God forgive me, I didn't mean it.

"Of course not." Paul probably didn't mean that, either. "Go," he said. "Be inspired. I'll be right here when you get back."

Of that there was no doubt. My Paul was a *there* sort of guy.

"Speed through!" I said, gaily, waving goodbye.

With the sun high and white, I marched up the cobblestoned hill, bought a ticket, stepped through the giant carved wood door of the Alhambra palace and lost my breath. As the kings had planned. From floor to ceiling, every inch was decorated with swirling blue and yellow geometric tiles, plaster wall carvings as intricate as lace, horseshoe arches, eddies of wood inlay in vaulted ceilings, slender columns with capitals bursting in vegetal glory, engraved Islamic inscriptions. Spain's diverse history before my eyes. Not to mention the mind-blowing view of the Sierra Nevada and the whole of Granada below. I took a thousand pictures before racing back down the hill.

To Paul. My *there* kind of guy.

Chapter Eight

It was a heavenly ending to a divine trip. The smooth Andalusian highway was a straight shot to Granada's Federico García Lorca airport. With Paul at the wheel, we gave ourselves plenty of time to catch the flight. Cracking the window an inch, I inhaled the hot Spanish air.

"Do you have that map?" Paul darted a glance from the driver's seat.

"What map?"

"The rental-car guy gave us a map."

"I thought the airport was a straight shot?"

"It is. I think. I want to be sure. I haven't seen a sign in a while."

I checked the glove box, the center console, the backseat. Nothing. Our packed suitcases were stowed in the trunk. I bit down on a flash of impatience. If my husband hadn't known how to get to the airport, shouldn't he have made sure the map was in the car? Shouldn't we have ponied up the extra cash for a GPS? Or a prepaid cell phone with international service?

"I have to pee," I said, curtly. "Pull off at the next exit and I'll run into a café and ask."

Paul hesitated. A cliché male, he hated to ask for directions. Even when it was me who did the asking.

"Or we could take a leisurely drive to Gibraltar?"

In silence, Paul flicked on the blinker and crossed over to the far-right lane. At the next exit, he left the highway. He wound around a corkscrew loop that deposited us onto a congested street. Orange construction cones detoured traffic into a bottleneck. Horns honked. My bladder puffed up like an overinflated life raft, pressing against the nerves.

"There." With a waggling finger, I pointed to the first café I saw. Its sad chiffon curtains let me know we were on the outskirts of a town. A jackhammer pummeled the pavement nearby. The air smelled of tar.

"Crap. No parking," Paul said.

"Parking? Just pull over. I'll run in and run out."

A muddled look clouded Paul's face. Irritated, I snapped, "Shall I pee into the seat?" *Adiós* to my good mood.

Inciting a cacophony of horns and Spanish gestures,

Paul pulled into an alley next to the café and stopped. He rose both eyebrows at me as if to say, "Happy?" Then he pointed to a sign that read, "*No estacionar.*" No parking. Already out of the car, my hands flew into the air.

"Circle around, then. I'll be out in five minutes."

Leaving my purse on the floor of the passenger seat, I ran for the entrance to the café. A bell jangled on the glass door. Inside, the air smelled of steamed milk.

"*¿Baño, por favor?*"

"*Solo para clientes.*" The young woman behind the high counter regarded me blandly. She had a possum face with tiny features crowded into the center of it. Eyes large and round and black. There was only one customer in the café, a man hunched over greasy fried eggs.

"Espresso, *por favor.*" A small price to pay for a (hopefully) clean bathroom. The possum flicked her head toward the stairs. I took them two by two. Without taking the time to lock the bathroom door, I unzipped my jeans with hands flapping like a hummingbird's wings. Yanking down my underpants, I landed on the toilet at the exact moment my bladder let go.

When I returned downstairs, relief flooding my face, a miniature white cup on a coaster-sized saucer waited on the glass counter. A curl of lemon peel sat like a piglet's tail beside it.

"*Muchas gracias,*" I said on the exhale. "*¿Cuánto cuest—?* Oh.*"

Only then did I remember that my purse was still in the car. "*Mi,* um, wallet, *con mi marido . . . en el coche.*" I pointed outside. "*¿Momentito?*"

The possum shrugged lazily. "Life," she seemed to say in her Spanish way, "isn't as serious as everyone makes it out to be."

Leaving the espresso on the counter, I hurried outside.

Paul wasn't in front. I turned to look in the alley. So vivid was my expectation of seeing him idling there, I could feel the heat of the chrome handle on my curled fingers, hear the hyena cry of the car door as it swung open, smell the refrigerator cool of the air conditioner.

He wasn't in the alley, either.

Traffic rumbled past. Sunlight bounced off oncoming windshields. I stared down the one-way street, listening for a tooting horn, watching for the flash of a waving hand.

Our rental car was white, wasn't it? Or was it a light gray?

The Spanish sun bore down on my head. I was wearing airplane attire: loafers, cushioned socks, jeans, a thick long-sleeved shirt. Flying always made me cold. Now, sweat prickled my back. The shadow of a headache lurked behind my eye. *Are you kidding me?* Two weeks of guzzling red wine and I get a headache now? Before a transatlantic flight?

The possum stepped over to the café window, her expression cloudy with suspicion. I slapped one hand over my heart. "*Lo siento*," I called out. I raised my forefinger and repeated, "*Momentito.*" A full euro tip for her, I thought. Maybe all of our excess change?

If Paul didn't get there soon, it would be too late for me to take the sumatriptan I had in my purse. In this heat, a headache could morph into a migraine in minutes. I had to catch it before it grew beyond the point of no return. Judge Paul Agarra was so damned law and order, he was unable to park in a no-parking zone for five minutes? Didn't the *policía* have better things to do than ticket a husband waiting for his wife to pee?

Anger began to roil like lava. Where the hell was he?

Is that him?

That's him!

No, that's not him.

In two-minute increments, I waited. *Is that him? No. Damn.* I racked my brain for the make of our rental car. Golf? Or had I seen the Peugeot logo? It was a lion, right? Or was it a bear? Rubbing the pulsing vein on my temple, I beat myself up for not paying attention at the rental-car desk. When did I become a woman who blindly followed a man?

Fifteen more minutes passed, then twenty, then thirty. Then, who knows how long? Spikes of pain jabbed at my temple. Fear overtook my anger. With each passing moment, I felt sicker. Something awful had happened. Sometimes you just know. If Paul had a flat tire, he would fix it and show up; if he smashed the car, he would leave it for the tow truck and show up; if he felt dizzy, he would stumble down the sidewalk and show up; if he had a heart attack, he would wake up in the emergency room, yank out his IV, call a cab, leave the hospital in his flapping gown, and show up. My husband would crawl on his hands and knees to get to me. Never would he leave me standing on a corner unless he was unconscious or worse. Of that, I had no doubt. None.

My job was to stay put. Be the constant variable.

I watched. I waited. My headache was gone. In its place, the dark tentacles of a migraine wrapped themselves around the veins in my temple and squeezed. A sucker on one of its pointed tips attached itself to the back of my eye and pulsed like a festering sore.

Chapter Nine

Panic engulfed my body. My whole head hurt. Frantic instructions flew through my mind: call Isaac, call John, call Pet Camp. Nearly two hours had passed. We'd missed our flight to Málaga. Soon, we'd miss the flight home. I'd already dashed into the café to ask the possum to call the police. "*Mi marido*," I'd sputtered, trying not to burst into panicked sobbing. "*Él es sesenta y siete.*"

Sesenta was sixty and *setenta* was seventy, wasn't it?

The possum nodded and I ran back outside.

Is that him? No. *Him?*

John should be informed, shouldn't he? Would he fly over from Boston? Should I ask him to? Would he call his mother? I could picture Brenda stomping into Spain in her Birkenstocks, smelling of lotus incense. She would make it all about her.

"Whenever Paul and I traveled, we spent time *together.*"

In a sickening realization, I remembered that John's number—along with everyone else's—was in my phone, in my purse, in the car where my husband was probably trapped, waiting for the jaws of life. What the hell was the name of John's company? Something Interface? Acid churned in my gut, burning waves of dread. I was an awful stepmother. A terrible wife. Bad things happened to people over sixty. Did Spanish hospitals take our insurance? How could I contact anyone without money, a credit card, a passport?

My migraine jabbed at my face like a stiletto blade.

Just then, red lights flashed in my eyes. A blue-and-white police cruiser pulled into the alley and stopped. Two male officers stepped out. I ran to them. In a jumble of Spanish and English and some accidental French, I explained what had happened. We were on our way to the airport, I had to use the bathroom. My husband was circling around. He was hurt. We'd missed our flight. I'd been standing on that corner for hours.

They stared as if they didn't understand.

"*Tengo,* um, um . . . fear. *¿Una* heart attack, *peut être? ¿Accidente?* Hospitals?"

"*¿Se fue al aeropuerto?*" The older of the two officers crossed his arms in front of his chest. They both wore cornflower blue shirts and black pants.

"Did he go to the airport? Is that what you're asking?"

"*Sí.*"

"No. Of course not."

"*¿Cuánto tiempo has estado casada?*"

I stared, baffled.

"Husband," he said in fractured English, "marry *muchos años?*"

"How long have I been married?"

"*Sí.*"

"*Veinte y dos años.* Twenty-two years."

"*¿Tal vez, él está con otra mujer?*" Now, the younger officer chimed in. He slid his sunglasses atop his thick black hair.

"*¿Otra mujer?* Another woman? Is that what you're asking? Has my husband run off with another woman? No! That's crazy. Something awful has happened. I know my husband. He would crawl on his hands and knees to get to me. *Por favor*, I'm begging you, please call the hospital."

The police radio attached to the older officer's shoulder crackled. He stepped away. I felt my veins grow cold. I braced myself for bad news. When the officer returned, he mumbled something to his partner then turned to me. "*Ven con nosotros.*"

"Come with you?"

"*Sí.*"

"You've found him?"

"*Sí, sí.*"

I gasped. "Oh my God. Is he alive?"

"*Sí. Ven.*"

Exploding into tears, I flung my arms around both cops. I waved at the possum who'd stepped out onto the sidewalk. I pressed my palms over my heart. A gesture that I hoped said "Thank you" as well as "I'm sorry for not paying for the espresso." I hadn't touched it. Could she reheat it for the next customer? Use it for a *cortado*?

Scrambling into the backseat of the police car, I bit the inside of my cheek to stem the flow of tears. Not that it did. My cheeks were shiny wet. My nose ran. I wiped my face and nose on my sleeve. I didn't care. My husband was *alive.* Even if he was paralyzed from the neck down or crippled by a stroke or in need of painful rehab, I would take care of him. If he needed my kidney, it was his.

"What happened?" I blubbered. "*¿Accidente?*"

The young officer swiveled his neck in my direction and said one word that would forever alter my marriage: *aeropuerto.*

"You're telling me he's at the airport?"

"*Él ha estado allí durante más que dos horas.*"

I didn't need a Spanish lesson to understand what the police officer was telling me: Paul, my man, my *there* kind of guy, had been at the airport the whole time.

Chapter Ten

Through a dirty window in the subterranean air-port police station, I saw my husband sitting in a vinyl chair drinking coffee from a throwaway cup that read *Saimaza*. My rolling suitcase rested beside his against the wall. My purse hung from the back of his chair. Tears spurted from my eyes as I pushed through the glass door and ran to him, slapping my hands over his body to make sure he was real. "Are you okay? What happened?"

We threw our arms around each other. I wept into the mossy aroma of Paul's shirt, the smell I thought would kill me if I never breathed it in again. "What happened? What happened?"

"Where were you?" Paul whispered into my hair.

"What?"

He repeated, "Where were you?"

When I pulled back, I noticed his dry eyes. The un-settling thought flared that he was working up tears. The way a baby does when he falls down and is more shocked than hurt.

"Where was *I*? What do you mean? I've been stand-ing on the corner where you left me."

Both police officers looked away. They were loitering in the background with the airport officers. Apparently, crime was low in Andalusia. The young officer quietly said something about the *otra mujer.*

"What happened, Paul?"

As abruptly as they'd started, my tears dried up.

"I tried to drive around the block," he said. "There was construction. A detour. It was impossible to get back to where I was. I figured the one place you knew I would be was the airport."

"What?"

"You know, because we had that flight."

"*What?* You left me and drove to the airport?"

"I saw the airport sign when I tried to circle around. So I followed it. Because I knew you would know I was there."

Unable to formulate words, I dropped both arms to my sides and stood with my mouth hanging open. Paul draped my purse strap over my shoulder and bent down to grip the handles on our rolling bags. He said,

"There are commuter flights every hour at ten past. If we rush, we can make the next one." He then rolled out of the police station without another word. I felt a cartoony sensation, as if I'd been whacked by a two-by-four and was vibrating back and forth. As if bluebirds were whistling around my head. Through the window, Paul waved me outside. He pointed to his wrist even though he wasn't wearing a watch. In an unstable gait, I followed him. The Spanish cops stared at me. Were they waiting for a tip? I spluttered, "*Gracias. Lo siento.*"

Regarding me with pity, the older officer said in English, "Cell phones. Not expensive."

Out the door I went, following Paul, my there kind of guy. Incredibly, his face was animated in a smile. "I told the airport police you were lost. That must be how they found you."

On that warm afternoon, I felt my body grow cold.

"Lost? I wasn't lost. I was standing where you left me."

We passed through the electronic doors into the airport. With purpose, Paul marched up to the ticket counter and said to the agent, "I found her!" To me, he said, "When I checked in to see if you'd boarded the plane, she was incredibly helpful."

"You checked in?"

Paul didn't answer. The female agent smiled and said, "I'm happy to see you're okay, Mrs. Agarra."

In a fog, I reached into my purse for my passport. Slowly, my brain began to process what I was hearing. While Paul bought two new plane tickets and chitchatted with the agent—"That Alhambra, what a sight. Have you been?"—I felt icicles form on my heart. I grabbed the handle of my rolling bag and pointed myself in the direction of the security line.

"Hold up, Fay." Paul jogged to catch up. "We both have pre-check."

The bright airport light hurt my eyes. By now, my migraine was part of me. As if I'd been born in pain and nausea and had known no other existence. In the short security line, I rubbed the stiff muscles in my neck.

"The rental car."

"It's okay," Paul replied. "I returned it."

"How much did they charge for the late fee?"

"Late fee?"

"It was due before one."

"It's okay. I made it in time."

I nodded slowly.

"My purse."

"I gave it to you. It's right there."

"You didn't see it on the floor by the passenger seat?"

"I saw it when I returned the rental car."

"On time."

"Yes."

"So, you knew then that I didn't have money. Or a passport."

Darkness descended over me. A slowly lowered blackout shade. Paul gaped, pug-eyed. "Don't you think I've been through hell? I pounded my hands on the steering wheel. I tried to loop around. Don't you think that tore me up? Why are you being like this? I said I was sorry. I tried to find you."

"No." My voice was spiked with ice shards.

"Yes. I *did* try to find you. I circled arou—"

"No, you *haven't* said you were sorry."

"Jesus Christ, Fay. Sorry. Happy?"

At that moment, I was certain I'd never feel happiness again.

How could my husband leave me?

I spoke not another word to Paul for the rest of our trip. My heart beat black blood. Somehow, we made it back to New York. With a whistle and a thud, the landing gear lowered itself into position. We bounced and screeched when the tires hit the ground at JFK. The back thrust of the engines pressed my body against the seat. For a moment, my migraine—still my sinister companion—was pushed to the rear of my head. I imagined kneeling before our toilet bowl at home, opening my mouth, and spewing bile.

As soon as we pulled up to the gate, I felt rage at the passengers ahead of us. Who decreed that disembarking passengers had to go row by row? If someone in the middle of the plane had no carry-on, why couldn't she dash off while others were yanking duffel bags out of the overheads? Who gave the airlines the right to hold us prisoner?

When, at last, it was our turn, I watched Paul clutch the seat back to pull himself up. He winced. Before he left me, I would have asked, "Are your knees still bothering you?" I would have cared. He would have said, "No," and I would have known he was lying. We would have performed our marital dance: the unspoken way we knew how to handle each other. It took trust to learn those steps. Faith to execute the intricate twirls. I never dreamed my Paul, my man, would drop me.

"What, you're never going to speak to me again?" he asked.

As I had rehearsed in my head during the ticking minutes of our long journey home, I stated, "Until you understand why it would never even *occur* to me to leave the corner where you left me, I have nothing to say."

Chapter Eleven

"You're going to end your marriage over this?"

Anita met me for a drink at Minton's, her favorite bar near her studio in Harlem. She was prepping for a gallery show; I'd skipped yoga class in favor of a tequila Blood and Fire and scallion fries. Since Spain, I'd been unable to paint. I kept reaching for blue black.

"No," I said, tightly. "Paul is."

"You've got to let him out of the doghouse," Anita said.

I shook my head no. "Until he understands why it would never even *occur* to me to leave the corner where he left me, I have nothing to say."

It became my mantra. My line in the sand.

Anita and I met in art school. From the start, everyone could see she was the best of us. Back then, she painted round women in a style similar to Kobayashi or Matisse, yet completely her own. Me, I painted houses with blank windows. My early inspiration was Egon Schiele.

Anita Pritchard was the sort of woman whose chin preceded her body when she walked. As confident as a backless dress. The line from the nape of her neck to her tailbone was I-beam straight. Even when no one was looking. Though someone always was. Tall and Junoesque, she had one of those boyish haircuts few women can pull off. White blond, long bangs in front, short buzz in back. Earlobes on display. Anita would never dream of hiding behind hair.

"Whoa," she said when she first blew into my corner space in the student studio. "I must have this." She was referring to one of my older paintings. A stylized portrait of a woman I'd seen on the subway. I liked that one, too. I flushed with pleasure.

"We'll trade." She swirled away. I followed her. Of course. Like a cyclone, Anita was a spinning mass of energy that sucked everyone into her warm core.

I remember every moment of that first encounter. Planting herself in front of me, Anita scanned my face, my body. She stood close enough for me to worry about my breath. Involuntarily, I crossed my arms high in front of my chest, as if I were standing there naked.

"Got it." She walked over to a bin of mounted canvases—already, she had done more work than anyone else—and flipped through. The wood frames *whap, whapped* against one another. I inhaled the earthy scent of oil paint, the citrus aroma of terpene. In one precise motion, Anita pulled out a portrait and held it up.

"From my family's trip to Cuba."

It was a painting of a middle-aged woman in a flowery dress. The *back* of her full body, as she walked uphill. Her black hair was unkempt in a provocative way. As if she'd just woken up. Her thighs still sticky from sex. Her rear end was wide and visibly rippled. Her bare elbows were cushioned in excess flesh. The painted woman glanced over her shoulder, facing the viewer. Her expression was a blend of annoyance and invitation.

"You'll like this one," Anita said.

She was wrong. I *loved* it. I didn't look at that painting as much as I fell into it. Instantly, I knew I would spend hours staring at the expression on that woman's face, studying how an artist could capture such a complex emotion so brilliantly.

From that day on, Anita Pritchard and I have felt like sisters. Or the way we imagined sisters feel. She's an only child; I only had brothers. Ours is an inexplicable closeness. Our cogs fit. In school and after, we shared an apartment, our fantasies of the future, our sorrows of the past. She was the maid of honor at my wedding. After all these years, I still feel lucky to be her friend. I'm so clearly out of her league.

"Another drink?" she asked me at Minton's.

"You read my mind," I replied.

Chapter Twelve

"Had my purse slid under the passenger seat? Is that why you didn't know I had no money? No credit card? No way to look for you?"

Sometimes a person has to speak to her husband whether she wants to or not. In the weeks after Paul and I returned home from Spain, I foraged for a plausible explanation.

"Was there a language barrier when you spoke to the airport police? Is that why you said I was lost, not you?"

Paul shrugged. Like he didn't care. "It wasn't *nighttime*, Fay. It's not like you were a two-year-old who lost her mommy."

I stood there, speechless. My upper lashes hit my lower eyelids with a *plink, plink* sort of sound.

"You should have put two and two together," he

said. "You should have known where I was. Where else would I be? You could have taken a cab to the airport and met me at the rental-car return. I would have paid the cabdriver then. Why are you making such a big deal out of this?"

Over and over, he squirted lighter fluid on my smoldering upset.

"Let it go, Faith. Christ."

Since when did he call me Faith? Since when did my law-and-order judge *swear*?

I waited for feelings of love to creep back in like fog. The way they always did after a fight. Always *had*, before my husband of two decades became a man I didn't recognize.

Instead, things got worse.

It was a Saturday. On the cusp of fall, the air was pleasantly cool. I woke up content enough. Sometimes a person has to get over things. Next to me, Paul's stomach rose and fell. He snorted the guttural sounds of his sleep. *Mmkaw.* Lola sat on the rug below my side of the bed, staring at me with the stillness of a lioness waiting for a gazelle to wander over. I got up, fed her, and opened the back door to our garden. "We'll go to the park later," I said.

The Spain Incident—TSI, as I'd come to call it—had softened into a remembered sting. A wasp wound from childhood. My husband had made a mistake. Whose husband hadn't? I knew he was sorry. Not everything had to be put into words. That's what I told myself. Sometimes a person has to move on. So I did. Upstairs to the kitchen.

The smell of sizzling butter woke Paul up. In his robe, he clomped up the stairs to the kitchen. "To what do I owe this honor?"

"To you, Your Honor." I poured my husband a cup of coffee and added heavy whipping cream. His morning indulgence.

"Orange juice?" I asked.

"Splendid."

Bzzzz. Lola galloped up the stairs from the garden.

"Oh no." I considered ignoring the door. I plopped two misshapen pancakes on Paul's plate and turned back to the stove.

Bzzzz. Bzzzz.

Bark. Bark.

"Lola. Stop. Now."

Bark. Bark. Bzzzz. Bzzzz. Neither would give up anytime soon. "Paul." I, too, barked. "Can't you hear the buzzer?" He lifted his head and regarded me disinterestedly. When I stomped to the door, he reached for the butter.

"Yes?" I hissed into the intercom.

"Fay-*ee*."

As I knew it would, my heart sank. "Brenda."

Bark. Bark.

"Who else would be up at this ungodly hour?"

At the kitchen table, Paul smeared butter over his pancakes. He licked a drip off the syrup bottle.

"How can we help you, Brenda? So early. On a Saturday."

"Very funny, Fay." *Bark. Bark.*

"We're in the middle of breakfast." Truly, I wasn't in the mood. Not when I'd so recently retrieved my mood from the bottom of a well.

"Is your buzzer broken?" she asked, impatience tainting her voice.

Bark. Bark.

"Paul!" I shouted. "Shut Lola up!"

Without getting up, Paul tore off a piece of his pancake and threw it across the room. Lola scampered after it. I stared at him with my mouth open. Brenda yelled into the intercom, "For God's sake, Fay, let me in. I have an appointment."

Appointment?

"Let her in," said Paul.

My molars pressed together. Could he never tell that woman *no*?

I buzzed her in. I unlocked the apartment door and

left it open and tromped back to the stove thinking, *I'll be damned if I'm going to make Brenda pancakes. And Paul can get his own juice. So there.*

"Good heavens," Brenda said, breathless at the top of the stairs. "You'd think you live in Fort Knox."

Paul looked at his ex and asked, "Orange juice?" Then he said to me, "Fay? Juice for both of us?" I looked at him like he was out of his mind.

"No, thanks," said Brenda. "I can't stay. I just swung by with the paperwork."

"Paperwork?" I turned to face her.

"The loan."

"What loan?"

"Didn't Paul tell you?"

At that moment, Paul set down his fork, licked his fingers, wiped them on his robe, and calmly took the manila envelope out of Brenda's hand. As I stood there with a spatula in my hand, he pulled a contract out and proceeded to sign it.

"I had our lawyer draw it up," Paul said in the same breezy tone he used when he asked, "How are those pancakes coming? You only made two."

"Paul?"

"All set." He handed the contract back to his ex.

"*Paul?*"

"Yes?"

"What's going on?"

Tiptoeing to the door, Brenda said, "Whoa boy. Don't want to get in the middle of this." Quietly, she let herself out.

"What just happened?" My mouth dangled open.

"Bren borrowed money for something or other."

"A meditation studio?" I enunciated each syllable. *Med-i-ta-tion-stu-di-o.* It was the cockamamie plan she'd been hatching before we left for Spain. Before my husband left me on a corner and drove away.

"Something like that."

My free hand flew up to my head. My eyes darted around the kitchen. "Am I being punked?"

Paul raised his nose in the air. "Do I smell something burning?"

Chapter Thirteen

It was a gentle invitation instead of a dare. A *whoosh*. Not a *clang* or a *thunk*. When your elevator door opened, I heard Benny's mom say something with the cadence of a greeting. Benny resumed his yapping.

"Once we move in," I muttered to myself, "Lola will teach that Muppet some self-respect." At least my girl barked for a reason. Protecting her turf. What, Benny thought he owned the lobby? The elevator?

From my perch on your antique bench, I heard footsteps on your marble hallway. I saw his hand before I saw him. It slid down the brass railing of your interior steps and glimmered in a halo of reddish hairs. He wore a white shirt, tucked and belted into twill pants. Suede brogues. His shirt was rakishly open at the collar. One button, maybe two. I stared, unblinking, unable to turn away. All of a sudden, he looked up. Straight at me. Electricity surged through my body. Instantly, I absorbed the curls of his light hair—graying red? His glasses were tortoiseshell. His skin was pale and freckled. He smiled with the knowing warmth of a pediatrician. The sort of doctor who would circle around his desk to take your hand before he told you that your child had leukemia. A man who understood sorrow.

In his age and unhurried gait, I surmised that the pediatrician was semiretired. Six months out of the year he volunteered with Doctors Without Borders? Which, of course, he called *Médecins Sans Frontières* because he'd mastered French late in life to better serve the Haitian kids who so desperately needed his help.

"Hello," I heard myself utter as he drew near. My voice, I noticed, lilted with the faintest accent. I dropped the *H. 'Ello.*

"Hello," he replied. Openly, simply. Without the hint of an agenda. As he approached your front door, I watched the pediatrician pass under your central chandelier. In its soft light, he looked angelic.

"Morning," he said to Juan Carlos on his way out the door. Obviously, he was a man of few words, primarily a listener. I watched him descend your front steps and turn right, uptown, away from Lola's hydrant. Breaking my heart, he disappeared from sight.

As if watching a movie inside my brain, I saw it all unfold.

"Forgot my mobile," he'd sheepishly tell J.C., returning a minute later. Having only recently come home from Africa, he'd still call a cell a "mobile," a trunk a "boot," a garbage can a "bin," and sneakers "trainers." He'd say he was pissed when he was actually drunk. And it would sound charming, not fake like Madonna or Gwyneth.

Juan Carlos would shake his head. "Man, I lose my phone at least once a month." It wouldn't be true, but he'd make it sound as though it were. That's the kind of doorman—man—he was. He put others' needs first.

Once inside, the pediatrician would aim for your interior steps. His breath would catch when he sensed my presence. He'd stop for a millisecond before looking up. Then he would. Look up. My cheeks would flush pink. When our gazes met, I'd notice the diamond sparkle in his eyes. The sort of grin that changes a whole face.

"You're still here," he'd say. He wouldn't say, "I'd hoped you were," but it would be understood. As if pulled by a riptide, he'd float over to the antique bench. I'd see the slight shaving rash beneath his chin. I'd resist the urge to kiss it. To claim that fleshy spot as my own.

"May I?" he'd ask.

In reply, I would slide over. I, too, would be a person of few words. He'd like that. I'd watch the kaleidoscope colors from the stained glass windows shift from my right sleeve to my left. The pediatrician would sit close to me. He'd be unafraid to maintain eye contact. My heart would beat so hard it ached.

"I'm Preston," he'd say.

No. Too stuffy.

"I'm Drake."

Too rapper. Too English sea captain.

"I'm Blake."

Yes. Blake.

"Hello, Blake. I'm Fay." My accent would fall away. I'd be back to myself. Only softer. Prettier. Thinner.

When I held out my hand to shake Blake's, he'd cradle it as if my fingers were newborn birds and his hands were their nest. His fingernails would be clipped and filed. Cuticles as snowy as an orchid's anther cap.

"I feel your despair."

He'd whisper so softly I wouldn't be sure he said anything at all. Still, I'd feel it. Despite my best efforts, tears would rise up and spill over. The beautiful kind, not tears that produce snot. With the back of his freckled forefinger, he'd brush my tears away. First one cheek, then the other. His hand would smell like homemade soap. I'd want to grab it and inhale it but I wouldn't. Not yet.

"Everything is going to be okay."

That, I would hear clearly. Another large teardrop would roll like maple syrup down my cheek. "Really?"

He'd nod and smile. He'd pat my hand. Lovingly, not pejoratively. With a slight rub to it. The way a pediatrician would. He'd say nothing more. Words were superfluous. In his warm grip, in the golden light of your lobby, on your shiny antique bench in the reflection of the glass sky, I'd believe that my days of sorrow would cease. With the pediatrician's help, I would find myself again. The Fay I once knew and had forgotten to appreciate. I would survive this. Joy would again effervesce in my soul like champagne.

Chapter Fourteen

My Alhambra collection was stunning, if I may say so myself. Once I was able to see color again, I worked until I got it just right. When lamplight shone through the painted shades, it cast a sunset glow throughout the room. Exactly the way I wanted to remember Spain. My way of forgetting the bleakness of a husband who inexplicably leaves his wife standing on a corner. Yeah, I'd tried to move on. I'd also tried to squeeze into a size 8 shoe. Some things hurt even when you can live without them.

As I suspected, the intricate Nasrid borders elevated my work. Time-consuming, but worth it. My Etsy account was on fire.

I set the alarm for six in the morning. While Paul snored like a chain saw, I walked Lola in the cadet blue of a fresh day. We stayed out until I was sure Paul was up and dressed and on his way to court. Much longer than usual. Lola loved it. Seated like a sphinx at the base of a park bench, she glared at passing dogs, slowly licking her lips.

Think you can take me?

If they did, they were wrong. Off-leash, my muscular girl could outrun almost anything on two legs or four.

When I unlocked the door of our apartment and heard the silence, I felt the balm of relief. Time alone was the only way I could stop my head from spinning.

". . . so Anita brings him up to her studio and he buys, like, five of her paintings. A guy she met on the subway!"

A few nights earlier, Paul was sitting at the kitchen table, watching me make dinner. Rigatoni with garlic and oil. One of his favorites. I'd decided to cook our way back to normal.

"That's Anita for you," I said. "Luck and guts. I'd never have the nerve to promote my work to a stranger."

"A stranger?"

"Yeah, I know. It was dicey going into the elevator with a man she just met, but cameras are everywhere and Anita made sure Louie saw her."

"Louie?"

"The maintenance guy at ArtLoft. Remember the

guy we hired to change the valves on our radiators?
You know, *Louie*."

"Ah."

The aroma of freshly grated garlic twirled into my
nostrils. I set a small pile of it in a big bowl, poured
olive oil over the top, added a bit of salt and a table-
spoon of butter, and covered the whole thing with the
steaming pasta. In two minutes, it would be ready to
toss and cheese and eat.

"Plus, her floor is full of artists," I went on. "She
wasn't bringing a stranger up to an empty space."

"What stranger?"

"The art patron she met on the subway."

"What subway?"

I gaped at him. "Haven't you been listening?"

Brushing me off, Paul said, "I'm wiped out." He
stood unsteadily and clomped down the stairs. The
ocean waves of our nighttime sound machine filled
the apartment with their ebb and flow. Stupefied,
I heard Paul groan as he settled himself into bed. It
wasn't the first time he'd done that. While I was making dinner! I couldn't believe my eyes and ears. Who
was this stranger living in my house?

So, I painted. All day, every day, I painted and
painted and painted. I told Paul, "I'm swamped," to

explain why I didn't answer my phone, why I stopped making dinner every night.

"Thai?"

"Whatever you want," he said.

"Thai it is."

Dinners landed on the table in white paper bags with menus stapled to them. The *PBS NewsHour* captured our focus while we ate. My nightly glass of wine—a heavy pour—made me sleepy enough to retreat to our downstairs bedroom the moment Judy Woodruff signed off. Paul filled the dishwasher and set the timer on our morning coffee.

From the sink in our downstairs bathroom, I listened to my husband's shuffle across the living room rug overhead. The aerosol spray of the Pledge he used to shine our dining table floated a lemon scent my way. He ran the garbage disposal and popped a dishwashing pod into the dispenser. All the tasks that once made me glow obnoxiously.

"Paul and I have the perfect division of labor," I'd brag to friends.

My comeuppance was now the scuffing of his shoes across the rug. Could he never pick up his feet? Did he have to sound so lunkish? Lately, I heard the coffeemaker grind in the middle of the night.

There, in my bathroom mirror, I ignored the irritation that was etched on my face. I brushed my teeth and washed my face and wore unsexy pajamas and climbed into bed before the clock ticked to nine. I marveled at the way our once overflowing marriage could run on empty.

"Feel like Mexican tonight?"

"You pick."

"Mexican it is."

We chewed and swallowed and drank wine while we watched TV. On weekends, we read the morning paper from beginning to end. I did laundry; Paul swept leaves in the back garden. I walked Lola during the day; Paul took her to the park after the sun went down. Each night, in the lonely island of my bed, I told myself, "Tomorrow will be back to normal."

Chapter Fifteen

Who could imagine such luck? An open house beyond your glossy front door. Unfettered access to your marble hallway, polished railings, interior stained glass, elevator. I was exhilarated. From one to four, that very day, everyone was invited in. My favorite word when it came to you. "In." Not left out. Not left, period.

I settled on the same outfit I'd worn before: Spanx jeans, a (slightly wrinkled) Brooks Brothers blouse, periwinkle mesh sneakers from J.Crew. The diamond stud earrings Paul had given me years ago. Hopefully, Juan Carlos wouldn't remember my look. More than anything, fall's chill worried me. My outfit definitely had a summer vibe. Perhaps I could let it slip that I'd just flown in from Aruba?

With the wind gusting east from the Hudson River, I thanked the universe for the rosy glow it gave my cheeks. Not to mention the rakish chaos it whirled into my hair. Exactly the windswept look that suited an apartment with an unobstructed river view. Leaving Lola at home, I made my way to the wonderland of Hudson Crescent.

"J.C.!" I trilled inside your vestibule. "Lovely to see you again."

Juan Carlos was momentarily thrown, but he covered it well. As any doorman worth his tuxedo-striped pants would. Helping him out, I said, "I'm here for the open house."

"Ah." Reaching inside his podium, he retrieved a form. "Basic information," he said.

"About what?"

"Name, current address, contact information, the usual. You know, for the real estate agent."

"Of course." In the excitement, I'd forgotten that someone would try to *sell* me the apartment I was there to snoop in. "Excuse my brain fog. I just jetted in from Aruba."

Smiling noncommittally, Juan Carlos handed me the form. "The open house begins at one."

"Yes. I know."

"It's twelve forty-five."

"Oh." A giggle burped through my lips. "Still on Aruba time!"

Afraid that Juan Carlos would make me wait outside on your cold granite steps—where I'd seen dogs pee (not Lola, not ever)—I swallowed my nerves and barged in. "I'll wait on that bench over there." To my delight, he stepped aside with a princely sweep of his hand.

Oh happy day. Once again, I was "in."

I chose to tell the truth. Sort of. I wrote my real name and address on the form. Though I jotted down a fake cell number. As I usually did. Did anyone actually *ask* Apple to tether us to everyone else every minute of the day? Flicking an angelic smile in J.C.'s direction, I set the completed form aside and sat back on your antique bench to let your beauty and calm wash over me. Silently, I prayed that others would show up. I wanted the real estate agent to be occupied. After all, the open house ended at four. A mere three hours to meander through your airy rooms, gaze out your sun-flooded windows, trail the backs of my fingers along the cool quartz of your kitchen countertops. (Not granite. Too yesterday.) If—please God—the real estate agent was busy elsewhere, I'd steal a moment to recline on the bed in the master suite. Provided, of course, the apartment was staged. The StreetEasy ad had only shown photographs of your stunning lobby.

"Hello." A woman's voice startled my eyes open. "You're here for the open house?"

"Yes." Too eagerly, I leaped up. *Chill, Fay, you idiot.*

"Sit. Please. It's not quite one o'clock."

I sat. With deliberate calm, I filled my lungs and slowly blew air out through my nose. As if I were in yoga class. "Let" on the inhale, "go" on the exhale. Jana, my yoga teacher, lovingly rested her hand on my back whenever my letting go produced tears. "It's okay," she whispered. Though nobody else cried in class.

"I'm Eve." The real estate agent reached out her manicured hand. A wave of horror shot through me. My nails were a mess. Ragged bits of skin jutted out from the sides of each nail. How could it not have occurred to me that someone might want to shake my hand? Fool. Could I pretend I had arthritis? Adopt a downtown swagger and move in for a fist bump?

"Fay," I said, locking eyes with Eve like a serial killer. I reached my right hand up, grasped hers, and pumped it once. Then I crossed both arms in front of my chest, tucking my fists into my armpits. The worst possible pose for the lighthearted look I was going for, but a poorly groomed girl's got to do what she's got to do.

"Welcome," Eve said. Her cheekbones were two hard-boiled eggs. Her complexion was whipped cream. Unable to stop myself, I stared, spellbound. Her blond hair literally *cascaded* over her shoulders. Clearly, it had been expertly coiled around a curling iron. She wore a Tiffany kiss on a delicate chain around her neck. The shiny silver X nestled into the hollow between her clavicles. Her lipstick was an indescribable color between pink and orange and red. The color I was always looking for, but could never find. Not in the drugstore, anyway. Almost certainly it had a name like Desire or Rapture in the Afternoon. Or something cool and cryptic like Torn. Eve had applied it with a brush, blotted, then brushed it on a second time. I could tell. It had that professional look.

"May I?"

Without waiting for an answer, Eve sat next to me on your polished bench. She picked up my form and read it. I inhaled the dry-cleaned scent of her linen suit. "You're looking for a one-bedroom?" she asked.

"I'm open."

"I see that you live in the neighborhood. May I ask why you're moving?"

Good lord, an *interview*? I felt a tad perturbed. What business was it of hers? Did she need to know how long I'd desired you? How I wanted to take our romance to the next level? With, hopefully, ice white appliances instead of stainless steel, which were so overused they were passé?

I considered blurting out the truth: My beautiful two-bedroom, two-bath duplex with sky-high ceilings, a wood-burning fireplace and private garden, in a hundred-year-old brownstone mere steps from Riverside Park, in which Paul and I had lived, loved, demolished, designed, painted, repainted, restored, and devoured countless pizzas on the floor with our backs against the wall, marveling at our ability to stay married during the stress of it all, was now a daily reminder of everything we'd lost. In every room, every exposed-brick nook, every bloom in the garden, I saw our past togetherness. I felt our union. How could I live with so many ghosts?

"Downsizing," I said.

"Ah."

At that moment, a young couple entered your lobby with both sets of their parents. Their faces were so hopeful I nearly burst into tears.

"Oh my *God*," the bride gasped. "This is, like, the most beautiful lobby I've ever seen."

I nodded in a proprietary sort of way.

Eve stood and clicked her impossibly high heels over to the newcomers with her posture perfectly erect. "I'm

Eve," she said, shaking everyone's hand. "Welcome. It's one o'clock. Shall we go up?"

My heart sent fresh blood to my face. I flushed in anticipation. Echoing my sentiment exactly, the young bride squealed. Her father, or maybe father-in-law, rested his hand on her back and said, "Let's not get ahead of ourselves." He was already negotiating.

Following Eve's toned calves, we ascended your steps aglow in the spill of light from a full *row* of interior stained glass. My expression was beatific. Such thoughtful design! So churchy. One couldn't help but feel blessed to be bathed in so flattering a light.

"Built in 1909 by the architectural firm Schwartz and Gross, the Renaissance style is reminiscent of their buildings in Morningside Heights."

Eve chattered all the way to your—manned!—elevator.

"Hello, Hector," she said. "Sixth floor, please."

I bit my lip. A doorman *and* an elevator man? I hadn't dared dream.

Up we went. All eight of us. Plus Hector. Your oak-paneled elevator gave us a smooth ride. No worrisome shimmy. I ran my fingers across my bangs as the doors swept open. "Sixth floor," said Hector.

Ridiculously, I winked at him. My body and mind had lost their connection. I followed Eve off the elevator and into the hallway. It smelled of fresh paint. Nothing unpleasantly pungent like Brussels sprouts or curried fish. Which didn't surprise me. A building like you would be populated with salad eaters. Vegans, most likely. If not, sippers of bone broth. Eve strutted down the carpeted hallway. I didn't bother craning my neck in hopes of spotting the pediatrician. I knew he would live on a higher floor. Not the penthouse, of course. Too ostentatious. Probably one floor below. Maybe two apartments combined? Bought in the eighties when prewars were a steal? Our tight group followed Eve to the far end of the long hall. There, she stopped and said, "Here we are."

With a twist of her wrist, she unlocked the door to apartment 6F. As if in a group hug, we shuffled in en masse.

It *was* staged. My heart hammered my rib cage.

"The parquet is original, an open layout . . ."

Clacking around in her spiky heels, Eve flipped on all the lights and chattered nonstop. Lemmings that they were, the newlyweds and their parents followed her lead. Not me. I peeled off and floated into the bedroom to take in the river view without distracting commentary. I'd gotten what I wanted. The real estate agent was busy with live ones.

Surprisingly, the gauzy white curtain over the lone

bedroom window was drawn. And the bed, a *double*, nearly filled the entire space. On my way past the narrow closet, I had to loop my leg around the footboard. A cushioned dining chair was nestled into a corner where an easy chair should be. It sat next to a leggy side table barely large enough for two paperbacks and an espresso. The stager had done her best. The puffy white duvet *did* look inviting. Still, there was no getting around the fact that the flat-screen television, mounted to the wall, was wider than the dresser below it. Had the StreetEasy ad mentioned a maid's room?

"Oh."

After sweeping back the curtain, I saw why it had been closed. The F line, apparently, was in the *back* of the building. With a view of pigeons pooping on a sooty ledge, breathing distance away. They cooed and flapped their wings around one another, trampling their own excrement.

I let the curtain fall shut.

"The cozy kitchen has a breakfast bar."

Following the sound of Eve's voice—and that dreadful real estate euphemism, *cozy*—I meandered out of the bedroom, down the dim hall to the microscopic kitchen. "Stainless steel appliances!" Eve chirped. "And a quartz countertop on the side cabinet!"

Side cabinet? When I leaned in for a closer look, I saw a disturbing sight. Clearly, the owners had bought a quartz *remnant* for the triangular end cabinet that was too shallow to be useful in any way whatsoever. Where would a person store her Cuisinart? Her Le Creuset Dutch oven? The soup tureen Mom gave me before she died? The one I'd never use and never part with? Compounding that blunder, the owners had committed a mortal sin: the main countertops were Corian, practically *laminate*. Nice try with the glass bowl of limes, Eve. Only a chump wouldn't see through that. Plus, the kitchen was so, well, *cozy*, it was impossible to imagine an actual meal being made in it. Sandwiches, maybe. Thanksgiving dinner? Forget it. Was the refrigerator even regulation size?

"Did you see the bathroom?" Eve asked me.

I hadn't. So, I swiveled around and made my way to the HGTV-styled bathroom. White subway tiles, shiny black trim, white cotton shower curtain, pops of teal accessories. I'd seen that episode in reruns. The style was clean and crisp. As formal as a tuxedo. Beautiful in a hotel sort of way. My heart broke as I imagined myself reclining in the soaking tub, surrounded by flickering candles. (White, of course, to match.) My hair would be coiled in a claw clip, soapy foam would cling to my manicured toes. I would be a movie scene, the one in which the single woman abruptly stops lathering her arm to call out, "Hello? Is someone there?"

Standing in that designed bathroom, I felt a riptide of sadness pull me home. I missed the cameo pink plaster walls of our master bath. The slightly raised spots where I'd spackled holes and not sanded them sufficiently, the cracked caulking around the tub that I'd been meaning to replace. I missed our floral shower curtain and the liner that got moldy around the edges when I didn't wash it often enough. The exposed heat pipe made our bathroom so toasty in winter; the towel rack my brother had built in front of it was inspired. Warm, dry towels all winter. I didn't want to buy shampoo in bottles that matched pops of teal. Not when I'd grown accustomed to a mismatched sort of life.

"Isn't it perfect?" With her hands clasped to her chest, the young bride stood behind me at the bathroom door, enraptured.

"Best address in the city," I replied, honestly, feeling a ripping sensation in my chest. Suddenly, I felt as though I'd never be happy without a toilet that needed a jiggle to stop its running and an old tub with a grip bar that looked like a ballet barre for Paul to hold tightly while I helped his skinny body into the bath, asking, "Warm enough, my love?"

Chapter Sixteen

It started with a pain in the neck. I remember that distinctly because when Mom said her neck was sore, Dad quipped, "Julia, you've always been a pain in the neck." My brothers and I laughed. Joey, the younger of the two, who was still five years older than me, said, "Faith is a pain in my *ass*."

"Language, Joey." Mom swallowed a smile.

"That's no way to talk to your sister." Dad was the sterner one. "Apologize, Joseph."

"Sorry."

I rolled my eyes. It was so obvious that Joey was so not sorry. He was never sorry for anything. Not the time he sold my bike to a neighborhood kid, not the time he spied on me through the lock hole in the bathroom door, not the time he told my parents I was asleep in the far backseat when they drove off to Disneyland

without me. Weren't older brothers supposed to pro-
tect you?

Nathan, my other older sibling, scraped his chair
back and stood up.

"I don't remember excusing you, son."

"May I please be excused?"

"Dishes," said Dad.

Nate's teenage shoulders slumped. "It's Faith's turn
to clear."

"Nah-uh. I cleared yesterday." My sneakers kicked
the leg of the table. I jabbed my tongue at him.

"It's Cubs against Dodgers, Dad."

Joey leaped to his feet. "May I please be excused?"

"Go."

Joey dashed to the den; Nate stared at Dad with
his thick eyebrows high. When Dad didn't relent,
my brother noisily stacked the dirty dishes, silver-
ware jutting everywhere, and grumbled his way into
the kitchen. All the while, Mom sat slowly rubbing
the side of her neck.

My dad and my brothers would remember that night
for an incident that happened in Dodger Stadium. It
was the bottom of the fourth inning. Two protesters—a
dad and his son—stormed the field with an American
flag they set on the grass and tried to light on fire.
Rick Monday, the Cubs center fielder, sprinted over

and snatched the flag before a flame could ignite. The crowd went wild. Dad talked about it for days afterward.

"That kid is from Arkansas. What a patriot!"

At Dad's office, they labeled Mondays, "Patriot Day," though it was pretty much an excuse to drink beer at lunch.

After that night, Nathan became a Cubs fan. Joey, too. But I remember that evening for something else entirely. It was the night my mother began to leave us.

For months, she walked around stiffly, as if her head were attached to a block of wood. When she turned to answer a question, she swiveled her entire torso. Nobody questioned it. At least not deeply.

"What's up with your neck?"

"Pulled a muscle."

"Hot water bottle?"

"Yeah. Thanks."

The sight of that red rubber blob on Mom's neck became our normal. As did her frequent disappearances into a hidden corner of the backyard. No one ever acknowledged the smell of cigarette smoke in her hair, on her hands, woven into the threads of the cardigan sweater she draped over her shoulders even when it was broiling hot outside. The California sun, she would say, was never hot enough to warm her through and through.

"I need a vacation in Hawaii."

The whole family would laugh. The closest we'd ever come to a tropical retreat was a picnic table under the craggy palm trees in Echo Park. The ones with the roof rats burrowed in them.

Almost imperceptibly, Mom's voice lowered. Bit by bit, she sounded husky, nearly male. The strip above her upper lip wrinkled into a picket fence. An earthquake rumble cleared the depths of her throat. She drank water constantly to help food go down. I can still picture her hand resting on her clavicle, as if she were trying to contain the spreading cancer between her thumb and fingers. I remember the orange stain beside her middle cuticle and the peppery smell of the Opium perfume she sprayed to mask her habit. It blended harshly with the Binaca she kept in her sweater pocket at all times. Two quick taps on her tongue when she thought no one was looking. But I always was. Most memories of my mother are stolen sightings infused with the scents of her addiction and its cover-up.

I suppose I should have been angry at my father for letting my mother deny her illness for so long there was no hope of a cure, only horrid treatments that left her too weak to vomit in the toilet. Or for all the lying he did.

"Mom caught a bug from one of the neighbor kids."

"Your mother is losing her hair because she doesn't eat enough foods with vitamin E."

Back then, the words "lung cancer" were uttered only in a whisper, followed by a bitten lower lip and watery eyes. Friends of the family would squeeze Dad's shoulder and ask, "What can we do, George?" Their conversations fell off a cliff whenever my brothers or I wandered within earshot. No one ever asked us what we needed, what they could do to help us cope with the disappearance of our mother before our very eyes.

I suppose I should have blamed my dad. But I never did. After he corralled us together—my brothers and me on the couch; Dad on a hard chair in front of us; Mom, pale as a full moon, swathed in an afghan on the recliner off to the side—to tell us what we already knew, I didn't get mad at him at all. Not even after Mom was gone, when he drowned in Budweiser and self-pity. Not when he allowed my brothers to raise me.

"Doing dishes is a girl's job," Joey decreed. "That's the new rule."

At no time did I feel upset at my father for coming through the front door after work and heading straight for the fridge. The *pffft* of his beer's pop-top didn't ignite my anger. Nor did his weeping or his plop on the couch and the drone of dire newscasts: "Toxic gas leaks kill thousands in India."

My distress was reserved for one person: Mom. How could she be so careless with a life I desperately needed?

How could my mother leave me?

How could the man who knew me better than anyone else—my Paul—not know that I would wait for him forever?

Chapter Seventeen

Sometimes a person needs a weekend away.

"Something is wrong."

A few nights ago, I came right out and said it. Despite the fact that Paul hated confrontation. Ironic for a judge. But enough was enough. The weirdness wasn't going away. Before he took Lola to the park that night, Paul had sneered, "What have you done with my keys?"

"I don't have them, Paul."

"I didn't say you had them, I asked what you did with them."

"Haven't seen them, haven't touched them."

"Oh? Did they walk away on their own?"

"Did you look in the bedside drawer?"

"What, you think I'm stupid?"

Flames flared in my gut. "No." I spoke with deliberate calm. "You're not stupid. But you're not yourself, either."

Lola was pretending to be asleep on her dog bed. I saw her lift one eyelid to look at us.

"Who the hell am I, Fay? Tell me. I'd like your expert opinion." Turning away from me, Paul stomped down the stairs.

"See? Right there. The Paul I know wouldn't be such a jerk."

"Name-calling. Nice. Lola, *come*."

Lola didn't move. She hated to be told what to do. Paul's foot hit the bottom step hard. He said, "Shit."

I said, "Something is wrong." What I didn't do was point out the fact that we'd had another silent dinner: Carmine's delivery, chicken scarpariello. Paul had seemed confused. Fork or hand? He'd looked at me with a beseeching expression that instantly broke my heart. In the next second, he looked away and grabbed a gooey, saucy chicken thigh with his bare hands. Instead of using a napkin, he licked his fingers one by one. His wineglass was so fogged with greasy fingerprints it looked like it had been processed at a crime scene. After dinner, Paul filled the dishwasher, but forgot to start it. Again.

Something was wrong. As his wife, I knew. Something had to be done. But what? From the downstairs hallway, my husband shouted up at me, "You're a doctor now? I thought you painted lampshades."

It landed like a machete in the center of my chest.

"Lola. Come. Now." Paul meant business. Lola knew it. She rose to her feet and tiptoed down the stairs to him. Bending over the railing, I yelled, "We have to talk about this, Paul."

"No. We don't."

I heard the jangle of Lola's leash and the crinkle of the plastic shopping bags Paul used to pick up her poop. With a slam, my dog and my man were out the door.

Yeah, sometimes a wife needs a weekend away.

"Kate?" I called Paul's daughter-in-law. John and Kate Agarra live in Newton Centre, Massachusetts, a forty-minute train ride from Boston. Two hundred miles from New York. Their daughter, Edie, is in high school. Though, seriously, Edie came out of the womb an adult.

"Mom is afraid to be still," Edie quietly told me one Thanksgiving. Her mother was in the kitchen with a crème brûlée blowtorch, caramelizing the handmade marshmallows on top of the organic yams. The rest of us were seated around her dining room table waiting for her. Edie was five. *Five.* What kindergarten kid has insight like that?

Brenda, Edie's other grandmother—the biological one—believes that Edie's body houses the reincarnated soul of Josephine Cochrane. The woman who invented the dishwasher. Like anyone's ever heard of her.

"My granddaughter was born to change the lives of women," she says, with proprietary pride. And, frankly, a touch of instruction. As if Edie's job is to fulfill her grandmother's promise.

"Or we could get men to do housework." That's what I said the last time Brenda spewed her edict. Which made Edie laugh out loud. I mean, the kid is in high school. Isn't being a teenager hard enough?

"What's up, Fay?" Kate asked me over the phone.

"I want to kidnap your daughter."

Kate laughed. "Shall I provide the blindfold?"

"No need. I want her to see where she's going. Ocean House. Girls' weekend with me."

"The spa resort in Rhode Island?"

"You know it? My friend Anita recommended it. It's only an hour and a half from Boston by train. I'll meet Edie at the station Saturday morning, then put her back on the train before dinner Sunday night. If she has homework, I'll make sure she does it between her mani and pedi."

Kate laughed again. Even though her pulled-togetherness makes me feel like a hair ball, I like her.

She has a core of kindness beneath her shell of control. It isn't always easy living with a husband like John.

"Boxed wine? Seriously, K?"

"It's a new thing."

"I like the old thing. Get rid of it."

I'd seen that exchange with my very own eyes.

Kate Agarra is one of those inexhaustible women who schedule Pilates class while everyone else is in REM sleep. She oils her cuticles in the hybrid SUV at stoplights and volunteers with a vengeance. When she thanks someone, she presses her palms together Namaste-style.

"Our daughter won't grow up thinking that success is a minimum of five thousand square feet," Kate had decreed when Edie was a baby and John got a job offer in Cupertino, California. "We are not living in Silicon Valley."

John, a coder, could work anywhere. He didn't much care where they lived. So the family moved to Newton Centre—a suburb of Boston—and bought a Georgian colonial with a circular driveway that was neither cheap nor small. We're talking a maid's *suite* on the first floor. It's that kind of house. Still, though Kate dislikes the pretentious spelling of "Centre," she likes Boston's feel of substance and permanence. It's so unlike the towns in northern California where the goal is making a kill-

ing at a meaningless dotcom that solves a problem created by another meaningless dotcom.

"If Edie doesn't jump at this," Kate told me, "I will."
She made it sound like a joke, but I knew she could use
a break from all that flawlessness she lugs around.

"Deal. If Edie says no, you and I will go."

Edie said yes. Which was what I'd hoped. She was
exactly what I needed: open, easygoing, the ideal distraction from the heavy marriage I'd been lugging
around lately.

Chapter Eighteen

Ocean House is a grande dame of a hotel. Perched
on a bluff overlooking the Atlantic, it resembles a
huge lemon-chiffon cake: multitiered, intricately decorated with white icing. Originally built after the Civil
War, it was restored to perfection a few years ago. The
croquet lawn and putting green are carpets of basil-
colored grass. Even in cold weather. The chef's garden
is bursting with herbs and exotic vegetables and fruits
no one has ever heard of like cucamelons. Ocean House
is the kind of stunning place that delights your eye at
every turn. Like the Alhambra in Spain.

"Oh, Fay." Edie's jaw dropped when she saw it. As
I'd hoped it would. It felt good to give an appreciated
gift.

Paul hadn't wanted me to go. I hadn't cared.

It was a weekend of chilling. In every way. The cold

air off the Atlantic reddened our cheeks when we were outside; inside, we ate spiced salmon on the heated terrace and drank champagne in the Secret Garden. Edie, of course, wasn't old enough to drink, but she was old enough to take a few sips of mine. I booked a detox facial, body polish, and deep-tissue massage. Edie chose the spa pedicure, organic facial, and an ancient sea salt massage, which, she admitted afterward, was a mistake.

"I'd just shaved my legs!"

We giggled and floated around in white robes and terry-cloth slippers. Saturday night, we ate popcorn and watched a movie in the hotel's screening room; Sunday morning we bundled into down jackets and strolled on the beach before brunch.

"Mom is making me crazy," Edie confessed. She knew she could tell me anything and I wouldn't tell a soul. Like the fact that her dad was rarely home. And her mom sometimes left the room when he was.

"She's always stressing about me deserving our family's good fortune. Like my SAT tutor—who I didn't even ask for—if I miss one session, Mom goes all Armageddon on me. 'Do you know how lucky you are to have a tutor? Do you know how many families can't afford one?' Sometimes I want to scream, 'Hey! It's not my fault Dad made us rich!'"

"Whom."

Edie turned to me. "Huh?"

"The tutor for whom you didn't ask."

Like Paul's, Edie's laugh was big and unabashed. "Okay, maybe I do need an SAT tutor."

Grinning, I hugged my granddaughter and she hugged me. As we walked, wet sand flipped into our shoes. We snuggled into our jackets and listened to the waves being sucked back to sea. We meandered in comfortable silence. After a long while, Edie quietly asked, "So, what's going on with Granddad?"

Quickly, I swallowed my surprise. "What do you mean?"

"Last time I saw him, he was, I don't know, weird."

"Weird? In what way?" As if I didn't know.

She took a deep breath. "I didn't want to say anything, Fay."

I stopped and faced her. "What happened?"

She bit her lip. "Well, we were walking in the park, you know, like we always do? All of a sudden, he gets this strange look on his face. Like he's lost. Then he asks me, 'Which way is home?' Like he doesn't know."

My heart fell to my knees. "That must have scared you."

"Yeah. I guess. Is he okay?"

Oh, how I wanted to open up. To spill the secret:

the craziness in our lives had multiplied like a flesh-eating bacteria. I hadn't even told Anita how strange things had become. How could I? Paul was a sitting judge. Livelihoods were at stake. Convictions could be overturned.

A few weeks before, in a restaurant on the east side, Paul had interrogated the waitress: "You mean to tell me, miss, if I get up from this table, and march into the walk-in, I won't find a single piece of branzino? Is that what you expect me to believe?" Then he reached across the table to take my hands in his. "You look beautiful tonight, my love."

A few nights before, after my attempt to reboot our love by making love, I whispered, "I want you to see someone." Near sleep, Paul grinned when he said, "You're right here. More convenient." It was something the old Paul would say, before he began to leave me bit by bit. I'd laughed. He did, too. Loud and full. The bellow I fell in love with. Up from the heart of the man I adored.

"Will you?" I'd asked, softly.

"Mm-hmm." He was more asleep than awake. I took a chance.

"I've noticed things, Paul. Ever since—" I mustered my courage. "Spain."

His eyes flew open. "Not that again."

"No, not that. Other stuff. I love you. Something is wrong."

Pulling away from me, Paul said, "Why can't you ever enjoy the moment? Why crowbar an agenda into everything? We'd just made love. You think that's the right time to bitch at me?"

His words were a slap in the face.

"Mind your own business, Fay," he snapped at me. As if my very own husband had nothing to do with me. Wobbling into the bathroom, he slammed the door.

Oh, how I wanted to confess to Edie that I was scared, too. But how could I? Edie only seemed like an adult. Paul would feel betrayed. He was her granddad, after all. She was his only grandchild.

"Big case," I lied. "They sometimes mess with his head."

With a slight shiver, I continued along the bubbly shoreline and steered the conversation toward safe subjects like the way a mother can drive a daughter nuts.

Late Sunday evening, when my key unlocked our downstairs apartment door, Lola ran to me, barking.

"It's me, you nincompoop," I said to her. Then I took her head in my hands and kissed her on her doggy lips. Calling up the stairs I shouted, "Paul? You here?"

"Lola?"

I sighed. I put my stuff on the bench at the foot of our bed. With Lola scampering ahead of me, I climbed the stairs and injected a breezy tone into my voice. "We had such a glorious weeken—" The sight of my husband silenced me. Paul's greasy hair was tornadoed all over his head, his white T-shirt was stained with smears of peanut butter. Gray stubble covered his chin and neck. He smelled foul.

"Did you sleep in those clothes?" A rhetorical question. I could see that he had. They were the same clothes he was wearing when I said goodbye Saturday morning. When I hadn't wanted to tell him how much I'd needed a break from him. How upset I felt at his inconsiderateness.

The TV was blaring. Cracker crumbs tumbled down the front of Paul's shirt. Remnants of peanut butter soiled his fingers. The open jar had peanut goo all over it. I could see peanut butter fingerprints on the refrigerator handle. My grown man—New York State Supreme Court Criminal Judge Paul Agarra—had used his fingers as a knife.

Yet, at that moment, seeing Paul sitting at our table like a grubby child softened me. The endorphins from Ocean House still flowed through my veins. He looked like a street kid, his belly round beneath his dirty shirt. I felt compassion. He was going through something.

Maybe it would pass on its own? It's what I wanted to believe, so I did. We would be "us" again. Forever anded: Paul and Fay.

Stepping close to my husband, I ran my hand over his warm, damp forehead and smoothed his wild hair. Gently, I asked, "How are you doing, my sweet?"

Paul's placid expression went black. "When the fuck are you going to stop taking my emotional temperature every fucking minute?"

Okay. Now it was time to tell.

Chapter Nineteen

"Isaac?" The next day, when I knew Paul's court-room was in recess for lunch, I called his law clerk.

"Fay." He picked up on the second ring. "How are you?"

My brain flip-booked responses: freaked out, gas-lighted, scared, pissed off, mystified.

"Fine, Isaac. How are you?"

"Good. Paul is out to lunch at the moment."

I nearly scoffed and said, "He certainly is." Instead, I adopted a Brenda sort of tone. "I was wondering, Isaac, have you noticed any changes in Paul lately?"

Before I confessed, I needed to know what Paul's work wife knew. Livelihoods were at stake. Convictions could be overturned.

He paused. "Like what?"

That pause spoke volumes. It was the sort of pause no one wanted to (not) hear. Like the Grand Canyon of air that would rush into a gap between "Do you love me?" and "Yes." I knew Isaac. He was a by-the-book type of guy. Chain of command and all that. As an officer of the court, it was his duty to make sure his boss was fit for the bench. A judge without sound judgment would have to be reported.

"He's on a new medication," I lied. "Nothing serious. But it has a few side effects. I've noticed a little—" I stopped. What could I say? He's mean, childish, clumsy? He swears?

"I'm sure he's fine." Isaac's tone was curt.

"So you haven't noticed anything?"

It was shorter this time, but I heard it nonetheless. The sound of silence. He said, "A muddy ruling here and there. Nothing reversible."

"He doesn't need a doctor, then? You know, to adjust his meds."

"I can cover for him."

Cover?

"Sorry, Fay, but I have to go. Big case."

I knew when someone was cutting me off. I'd used all possible methods with Brenda. Isaac didn't say anything more, and I didn't, either.

———

It's impossible not to question the inequities in the criminal justice system when you push through the revolving door of New York City's criminal courthouse on Centre Street. The line to the metal detectors is filled with people of color; their attorneys upstairs are nearly all white.

"Real estate," Paul once told me, by way of explanation. "White crime occurs inside, behind closed doors and curtained windows. Street criminals are out in the open."

"Remind me again: when's the last time the police raided a warehouse rave in Brooklyn?"

"I believe the term 'rave' is passé, sweetheart."

I'd laughed. "When is the last time the police raided an Ecstasy-fueled dance party full of white kids?"

"Duly noted." Despite its frustrations and flaws, Judge Paul Agarra believed in the color-blind rule of law. He understood the near impossibility of a kid rising out of poverty and despair when his parents—or single parent, or widowed grandmother—were too exhausted or indifferent to check homework. When dinner was microwaved mac and cheese, when teachers were forced to be cops, when cops were expected to be superhuman, when textbooks were so old there was no mention of 9/11 or Osama bin Laden or Guantánamo or Trump or the upside-down world in which we all now lived. Paul factored in the whole gnarled picture. He was known as the judge *both* sides wanted.

I decided to take a subway downtown and see for myself.

On the tenth floor, the elevator rocked to a stop. The doors opened onto a marble corridor dappled in sunlight. A woman, a mom, a grandmother, sat glumly on the long bench below the wall of windows.

"Always the moms," Paul often said, as if the fathers of the defendants hadn't the patience or loyalty to sit through a trial.

This high up, Tribeca was a checkerboard of beige rooftops. The windows were a thousand waffle squares. My hair could use a comb. My lipstick was faded. Still, I hurried past the mom and the restroom on my way to the far end of the hallway, hearing my boots clack on the shiny floor. Paul's courtroom was the last in the line, behind two sets of double doors: the first, painted black metal; the second, natural courtroom oak.

"So, you were wearing a metallic jacket that night? The night of February fourth?"

Recess was over.

"Yes," the defendant said. At least I assumed he was

the defendant. He wore a purple pin-striped dress shirt on the stand, open at the neck, freshly pressed. A lawyer sort of shirt.

"Purple? Are you kidding me, man?" I imagined the protest when his attorneys brought him clothes for trial. They, too, wore purple. Their ties. It was the modern color of defense. Not suggestive of a Blood or a Crip or a Latin King, not offensive to blue Democrats or red Republicans. The color of mourning or royalty in some cultures was now the American shade of presumed innocence.

"The same metallic jacket you're wearing in this video? People's exhibit 468 B?"

"Yes."

A juror turned his head toward me when I walked in and sat in the back row. Paul did not. When Isaac spotted me, I noted a faint look of alarm.

"A metallic jacket that's exactly the same as the metallic jacket worn by the victim who was shot a few blocks away, right?"

"Objection." A chair grated on the floor as one of the defense attorneys rose to his feet. "Assumes facts not in evidence."

All heads turned to the judge. My Paul. The Honorable Judge Agarra. Silence expanded like spray-foam insulation, invading every crevice. Paul's face was utterly blank. No affect whatsoever. His eyes stared into nothingness. My fists tightened around the strap of my purse. *Had my husband had a stroke?*

"Judge?" Isaac leaned close to Paul. The court reporter sat below them both with her fingers perched on the keyboard. It felt as if the square room had shifted into a rhombus. We all leaned forward. I saw Isaac subtly slide a piece of paper in front of Paul. *Dear God, don't let anyone else see that.* Robotically, Paul looked down and said, "Sustained."

The young man on the stand smirked at the jury. Attention reverted back to him. Paul seemed to come to. His demeanor was alert once more. "Don't answer," he instructed.

The prosecutor resumed direct examination. "Had you worn that jacket all night?"

"Whenever I was cold."

A juror burped up a laugh. Another rolled her eyes. I'd seen this many times before. In an attempt to highlight important evidence, prosecutors beat it to death. Usually, Judge Paul Agarra urged the attorneys to move on. Today, he sat high on the bench, mute. Usually, Isaac was busy researching case law, prepping documents, assisting Paul behind the scenes. Today, he sat at his side, nearly vibrating with a readiness to leap in.

In a deliberate way, I sucked air into my lungs and

forced it out through my nostrils. I didn't trust my auto-
nomic nervous system.

"Did you leave your apartment in the Bronx wearing
that jacket?"

"I left from my girlfriend's apartment."

"Wearing that jacket?"

"Maybe I let her wear it. As a gentleman."

At that moment, Paul seemed to wake up from his
trance. He turned to the defense table and asked, "Will
you be contending that your client did *not* wear a
metallic jacket that night?"

"No, Your Honor."

"Then why are we belaboring this? Move on, gentle-
men."

While the prosecutor flipped through notes, the
Cheshire cat in the witness box flashed his dimples at
the jury. One of the jurors smiled back. Never would
Judge Agarra allow his courtroom to get so sloppy.
Never would Isaac let him.

Suddenly, Paul looked up. "My wife is here!" He
woke everyone up. Even the cocky defendant looked
startled. Both defense attorneys stood up to object, but
Paul waved them off. "Relax," he said. "Ten-minute
recess."

Upending all protocol, Paul abruptly stood and left
the bench, marching through the central aisle of the

courtroom—the same aisle we'd walked down on our wedding day—to my seat in the back. In Isaac's stricken expression, I understood that Paul may have just handed an alleged murderer grounds for appeal. Quickly, the bailiff sputtered, "All rise."

Everyone rose. When Paul reached my pew, he sat with his black robe billowing. "You're here," he whispered. "I knew you'd come."

Around us, people were in chaotic motion. The court officer stood close to the defendant, unable to handcuff him before the jury had a chance to file out. Few sights were more prejudicial than a defendant in cuffs. Another court officer quickly shuffled the jury out a side door. They craned their necks to see us. Paul bent over to kiss my cheek. In his angelic grin, I saw that he was unaware of anyone but me. He took my hand.

"My darling," he said, softly. "I've missed you so."

Tears rose into my eyes. "I've missed you, too, my love."

Vaguely, I was aware that the jury had been ferried out; the defendant was cuffed and escorted to a waiting cell, the lawyers circled into covens around their tables. Somehow, I saw it all without looking up from Paul's hazel eyes. I fell into the sage circle around his pupil, the caramel sheen of his iris. Those were the eyes I'd melded into when I promised myself to him for life.

"Stay," Paul said.

"I'm not going anywhere."

Tears dribbled mascara down my cheeks. Paul swiped it away with his fingertips. He gazed at me with love so pure I felt high. I pressed my palm against my chest to keep my heart from breaking into pieces.

Now I was sure. Something was terribly wrong.

Chapter Twenty

D r. Fletcher was a busy man. He made that clear. "Fifteen minutes, Fay," he stressed over the phone. "Truly. That's all I have today."

"That's all I need. Thank you so much."

On the way to his office, on the subway, I mulled over what I would say. How to frame it. I told myself not to cry. He was a busy man.

The doctor's midtown office was a twenty-minute walk from Columbus Circle. Fifteen if you really chugged it. I arrived ten minutes early. In the waiting room, I flipped through the current issue of *Architectural Digest*. I listened to the *swoosh* of blood pulsing through my ears. I wished I had taken a Xanax.

"Fay Agarra."

"Here." Raising my hand like a schoolgirl, I stood up. Unlike every other physician in New York, Dr. Fletcher was fanatically on time. If you weren't willing to respect him in the same way, the office manager would politely hand you a list of referrals on your way out.

A medical assistant escorted me down a long hallway. She smiled blandly as I blathered, "Usually it's *People* in a waiting room. Or *Good Housekeeping.* You know, articles about brain-eating amoebas lurking in your neti pot?" I tried, but I couldn't stop babbling. "Interior-design photos are so staged. Like, who has fresh flowers in their bathroom?"

Dr. Fletcher's office was tucked into the corner at the end of the hall. His door was open. Following my escort's gesture, I entered the office and sat down. I tugged my skirt over my knees.

"Yes. Good."

He was on the phone. He nodded once at me. After the assistant silently backed out of the room, I purposefully lowered my shoulders. I positioned my head in a confident way. Chin up. The way Anita would. I settled into the down-cushioned chair. Unlike most physicians who hire a decorator to neutralize their turf with varying degrees of taupe, Dr. Fletcher's office reflected his personality: overstuffed, bookish. A coaster sort of space.

"Okay, then."

Abruptly, he hung up. *Whatever happened to good-*

bye? With his hands folded neatly on the desk in front of him, Dr. Fletcher fastened a half smile to his lips. "Fay. How may I help you?"

"It's Paul."

"Let me stop you right there," he said. "I can't discuss my patients."

"Of course. It's just that, well—"

Impatience was etched on his face. Coolly, he said, "I was under the impression that this consultation was about you."

"It is. Sort of. I don't know where to turn."

"Are you ill?"

"No. It's Paul."

He pressed his lips together in a prissy way. It's why I was no longer his patient. Paul loved him because he was the best. I switched to another internist after my first appointment because I felt like a naughty child in his presence. As if my cholesterol numbers were the wrong answers on a math quiz. "Something is off with him, Dr. Fletcher." My chin began to wobble. I clamped down on my teeth.

"Why isn't *he* here?"

"He thinks he's fine."

"Fay—"

"You promised me fifteen minutes." Magenta flared in my cheeks. "I am paying for fifteen minutes."

Stone-faced, he replied, "You have ten left."

Quickly, I plucked a tissue from the box on his desk and undaintily blew my nose. "When I ask Paul to empty the garbage, a minute later he'll forget."

In response to Dr. Fletcher's "Seriously?" face, I hurriedly added, "That's a stupid example. Garbage and husbands, I know. There are other things. Lots. Sometimes, when I talk to Paul about my day, he seems to be listening. I mean, he looks at me and nods. But then he'll ask a question that indicates he wasn't following the thread at all. He got lost in the park. In Spain, my God, his judgment was insane. And he's a judge! Over the weekend he was supposed to take our dog to the vet and he just *walked* her. When he came home, I asked him, 'Was it a tapeworm?' and he said, 'Was what a tapeworm?' Instead of taking her back to the vet, he plops down in front of the TV! His personality has changed. Not always, only sometimes. He swears. He never swore. My head is spinning. I feel like an alien has abducted my husband. Sometimes he's there; sometimes he's, um, mentally meandering. Like he's a *visitor* in his own life. Our mailbox is full of thank-you notes from obscure charities he gives money to. I'm worried about him on the Internet. All those scam—"

"Stop." Dr. Fletcher held his palm up. "You've said enough."

"It's hard to nail it down to one particular thing. It's a lot of little things. He's not himself. As his wife, I know."

"I'm sorry, Fay, but I really do have to end this meeting."

Meeting? Wasn't I paying for an appointment? I wiped my nose with the wad of tissue and blinked.

"I'll talk to him at our next appointment."

"Shouldn't he come in earlier, Dr. Fletcher? His physical isn't until next year. What am I supposed to—?"

In what struck me as annoyance, the doctor said, "Let me refer you to a good therapist."

"I don't think it's psychological. Neurological, maybe? At first, I thought he caught some bug in Spai—"

"For *you*, Fay." He wrote a name and number on a pad and tore it off with a flourish. "Thank you for stopping by."

"Wait. What?"

"Danica?" He pushed a button on his desk phone. "Is my next patient here? Good. Send her in."

With that, Dr. Fletcher held out the therapist's name and stretched his lips into a fake smile. I stood up and left empty-handed, without bothering to say goodbye.

Chapter Twenty-one

John didn't pick up. Surprising, since his phone lived in the palm of his hand. Nonetheless, I left a message. "It's Fay. Call me when you have a minute, okay? Nothing dire, but important. Talk soon."

Five minutes later, John called back. "Are you here?"

"Where?"

"Where. In Boston. Where else?"

"Why would I be in Boston? I'm in New York."

He groaned. "New York? You're going to miss Kate's dinner."

"What dinner?"

"Her *award* dinner. That philanthropy thing. Didn't Dad tell you? He said you both would come. We bought tickets for you at our table."

My head fell forward. "He didn't tell me."

"Ah, jeez."

"Is there a speech? Can we catch the next flight?"

"I'm on my way there now," John said. Then he cupped the phone. Through his hand I heard, "Shouldn't we take Cambridge Street? Skip the turnpike altogether?"

"I feel awful," I said. And I did.

"Sorry, Fay. Uber."

John groaned again, but it may have been traffic related because he sounded somewhat laissez-faire when he replied, "Kate will live." Horns honked in a commuter symphony. With an edge to his voice, I heard him inform the driver, "I usually head south on Chestnut Hill this time of day."

"You're busy. I'll call you tomorrow."

"No, no. I have a few minutes. You know how Boston rush hour is." As if the Uber driver might squeal on him, John said in a low voice, "Between you and me, Fay, it'll be one of those endless chicken/salmon events. Bad food, boring self-congratulations. Kate is embarrassed by the attention. I'll tell her something last minute came up." He stopped. "*Did* something come up? Is Dad okay?"

"Well—" In the same way I did a lot lately, I sucked in a full breath, held it for a moment, then blew it out audibly. *Bwoo.* I attempted to gather the bearings that were constantly escaping into the air around me.

John repeated, "What is it, Fay? Is Dad okay?"

"That's why I'm calling. He's been, um, strange lately. Not himself. Have you noticed anything?"

"Like what?"

"Forgetfulness, distraction, things like that." I didn't say, "He acts like a jerk sometimes, and a total baby, and he walks like a beginning ice-skater."

John laughed. "I suppose neglecting to tell you about Kate's award dinner is forgetful and distracted."

"Yeah. Again, ugh."

"Isn't Dad in the middle of a big trial?"

"Well, yes."

"I'm guessing that would consume a person."

"Yes, but—"

"And, let's face it, Fay. Dad is closing in on seventy. The wiring may be a little frayed."

"Of course. I get that. It's just—"

"Christ! Use your blinker, asshole! Did you see that guy? Christ!"

Even in a backseat, John experienced road rage. Paul had told him a million times, "It might help to remember that everyone else on the road is frustrated, too." Or he *used* to say that, back when he had empathy.

"You know when you know a person so well, you see things others maybe can't see?" Again, I inhaled, held it, blew it out. *Bwoo.* How could I tell him that his dad had morphed into an asshole? Not always, but enough to regularly piss me off. Enough to feel as though I'd been pushed down Alice's rabbit hole.

"Fay." John spoke quietly into his phone. On occasion, a whiff of superiority seeped into his voice. The same odor I sometimes smelled in his mother's treatment of me. "I've been wondering, Fay, how's your small business coming?" With an emphasis on the word "small."

John said, "Ever since I've known you, you've been worried about my dad. Am I right?"

The aroma of his condescension wafted through the phone. Nonetheless, it was true. The curse of marriage to an older man. Every pause in the trombone blare of his sleep is cardiac arrest, every cough is lung cancer, every bout of bad heartburn warrants a trip to the ER.

"I'm not sure what you're getting at," I lied.

"I talk to him on the phone nearly every week. He sounds fine to me."

"That's just it," I soldiered on. "He's fine sometimes, and not fine other times. On occasion, he goes blank. Not forgetful, *blank*."

John chuckled. "Yesterday, I blanked on Edie's teacher's name. There was a meeting at school—nothing negative. In fact, they want her to take one college class next year. Isn't that awesome? I sat in one of those student desks, all puffed up with pride over my brilliant daughter and I completely blanked on her teacher's name. I'm talking *air* blowing through my brain."

"It's not like that."

"Has Isaac said anything?"

I stopped. How could I tell what I'd seen in Paul's courtroom? Isaac's disturbed expression. His weighty pauses. Paul's bizarre behavior. A judge without sound judgment would have to be reported.

"Well, no. But—"

"There you go. Don't you think Isaac would notice if anything was wrong with Dad? You've said so yourself, they spend more time together than a married couple does. Isaac sees everything. He'd know."

"Well, yeah. But—"

"Fay." There it was again. The whiff. "Just because Dad isn't as sharp as he once was doesn't mean anything is wrong. Do you think it may be—I'm guessing here—your fears surfacing again? You know, like they have your whole marriage?"

"Do you think—I'm guessing here—that you're obsessed with work, to the detriment of your family? You know, like your daughter can see even though you try to hide it?"

That's what I wanted to say. But, of course, I didn't. I drew in another yoga breath and listened to John overdirect the Uber driver: "Or you could circle around the lake on Commonwealth."

"Please tell Kate how sorry we are that Paul forgot." I let the *f* word settle in John's ear. Forgetting to tell me about the award dinner is more than marital insecurity. Way more. John.

"Will do."

With that, he ended the call. John Agarra was never one to waste time with goodbyes.

Chapter Twenty-two

It's the "ifs" that haunt you. If it hadn't rained that night. If I'd trusted myself more, trusted white coats less. If I'd said, "Okay," when Paul said, "I'm not walking Lola tonight." If I'd done more research, been more forceful with what I knew to be true. If I'd spent less time in fear and denial.

If, if, if. If only.

It had rained that night. For hours. After dinner, after my heavy pour of wine, after I was in our bedroom and in my pajamas, ready to burrow into the crime novel I'd just bought, Paul stomped down the stairs and announced, "I'm not walking Lola tonight. She can shit in the backyard."

"Not fair." My voice sliced the air with its jagged edges. "You wanted an athlete. I wanted a corgi."

"One day. Big deal."

"And if it rains tomorrow. Two days. Or it's cold. Three days. Or your knee hurts," I added, meanly. I'd become my nagging father. *I should drive right over those bikes. That'll teach you!*

Lola sat perfectly still, facing the exit door. My yoga teacher would be proud. Our dog's entire being melded into the moment. No barking, no panting, no whining. Lola's silent expectation produced enough guilt to get what she wanted. Usually.

"I'll give her a bone," Paul said.

My face turned to stone. In silence, I exited our bedroom and walked up the stairs. In the reprimand of my taut back, I wanted my husband to feel the shame of denying Lola her nightly exercise, the disgrace of assuaging his guilt with food, as any bad parent would. At the top of the stairs, I stopped. I turned and stomped back down.

"I held up my end of the bargain." I revved up the argument. "I walked her this morning, in the rain. You think I wanted to get wet? You think I didn't want to give her a bone this morning? But I didn't. I did my *job* for this family. Grow up and do yours."

Sometimes, I couldn't stand to look at his face. The way his glasses slid down his nose. The greasy smell of his hair when he didn't shower. The leathery aroma of his work clothes. Disgusting.

Once again, I turned my back on my husband and marched up the stairs. I left him to prove to me that he was a man.

From my perch in the kitchen, arms crossed, staring out the window into the shiny darkness, I watched heavy raindrops hit the pavement like blobs of honey. I heard the opening and closing of the coat closet downstairs, the swoosh of the Patagonia parka I'd bought Paul back when he deserved such a loving gesture. Paul called out, "Come." Lola's toenails clicked across the wood floor to the door. She knew better than to test Paul's patience at that moment. I could picture her dipping her head to insert it into the harness, lifting her paw to slip it into the chest strap. My girl was so smart she knew how to get herself ready.

With a creak, the door opened. I heard them walk into the hall. Paul banged the door shut. I waited for the locking sound. Instead, the heavy *whomp* of the building's exterior door made its way to my ears. *He forgot his keys again*, I thought. *Idiot*. He probably forgot his phone, too.

I was glad he was gone. Happy he was getting wet.

If only.

It wafted through my mind that Paul and Lola had been gone a long time, but I discarded it like a used

Kleenex. The longer they stayed out, the more time I had to myself. Pandora blared from the TV. I danced while I tidied up. When the intercom buzzed, I felt annoyed. Did Paul even *try* to remember his keys?

"Yes?"

"Fay."

His voice was tiny. Like a child's. Instantly, fear kicked my stomach. As I buzzed Paul in, I opened the ground-floor door of our apartment. Down the hall, through the glass window in the building's entrance, I saw my husband's bloodied face. He tried to push open the heavy oak door, but couldn't. I ran to let him in. Lola slithered in first, her muddy leash snaking behind her. With a whimper, Paul said, "I'm sorry."

"My God, what happened?"

"Raccoon." His eyes glistened with fright. A rivulet of burgundy blood ran down his cheek.

"A raccoon attacked you?"

He shook his head no. I reached out to help him through the door and he yelped. That's when I noticed his shoulder. The right one, the same side as his bloody and swollen face, hung unnaturally low. And it jutted forward in a sickening sort of way. His hand, visible below the cuff on his parka, fell nearly to his knee.

"I'm calling 911."

"I'm okay." His teeth were stained with blood.

As if handling a tarantula, I gently guided Paul down the hall to our apartment, careful not to pressure any part of his body. His temple was split open; coagulated blood oozed beneath his chin. He shuffled through the door ahead of me. I ushered him into our bedroom and sat him on the bench at the foot of our bed. Lola was already inside with her head bowed and her ears flat. I didn't need to ask. It was obviously her fault.

"There's been an accident." The phone wobbled in my hand. My voice quivered. "My husband is hurt. His shoulder. His forehead. I'm not sure how bad. He's wearing a parka."

The 911 dispatcher's voice was calm. "Was it a car accident?"

"I don't think so."

"Is he conscious?"

"Yes."

She asked, "Can you tell me what happened?"

"We need an ambulance."

"Paramedics are on the way."

"Okay, thank you," I said.

"Don't hang up. Stay with me until they get there."

Perhaps he was in shock. Paul sat immobile. Fresh blood suddenly surged through the cut in his forehead and *drip, dripped* onto the floor. He had that vacant stare I'd seen before. My heart tumbled to my knees.

"It's all my fault. I was mad at him. I made him walk her."

"Walk who?" The dispatcher had the soothing tone of a kindergarten teacher. *Did you go boom-boom on the playground?*

"Our dog. I made him. In the rain."

"What's your name?"

"Lola."

"Take a deep breath, Lola. In and out."

"Fay." The harshness in my voice surprised me. "Sorry. My name is Fay. My dog is Lola."

"Okay, Fay. Take a deep breath. In and out. Can you do that for me?"

I vacuumed in a lungful of air. The dispatcher said, "Good, good. Now exhale." I blew it out with an audible "Ha."

"What's your husband's name, Fay?"

"Paul."

"Paul was walking the dog?" she prompted me.

"Yes. And something happened with a raccoon. That's all he said."

"Do you see a bite?"

I scanned Paul's bloody forehead for teeth marks.

Or the linear scratches of a raccoon's fingernails. "Did a raccoon bite you?" Shakily, I mimicked the 911 dispatcher's tone. *You have a boo-boo?* Paul stared up at me as if he didn't understand the question.

"I don't see a bite," I told the woman on the phone. I sucked in another breath. "Lola, our dog, probably lunged for it. Her face is all guilty. She had something to do with this, I know."

The dispatcher softly chuckled. A soothing sound. "My dog gets that look when she steals food from the kitchen counter."

Outside, a siren blared. "I think the paramedics are here," I said.

"Wait one more minute with me, Fay. Until they're inside with Paul."

"Should I go outside and meet them?"

"Stay with your husband, okay? You're in the garden apartment, right?"

"Right." Thank God for our landline.

At that moment, the buzzer rang. Momentarily, I was confused. "They're here," I said, uncertain of my next move.

"Is Paul steady enough to be left alone while you open the door?"

"Yes. He's just sitting there."

"Good. Stay on the line while you let the paramedics in. Okay?"

"Okay."

Dark blue uniforms were visible through the exterior door's window. Two paramedics. One woman, one man. Both younger than me. The flashing red of the ambulance light cast a hellish glow. *We must be alone in the building*, I thought. Otherwise, my neighbors would be gawking over the stair railing. When I buzzed the paramedics in, the woman entered first, her body leaning away from the weight of a rectangular box in her grip. Uncontrollably, I erupted in sobs.

"He's in here," I said, too loudly. To the dispatcher I begged, "Please let me go. They're here. I promise."

"Go," she said. "Good luck with everything, Fay."

I tried to thank her, but words were choked down my throat. I'm not even sure I hung up. Somehow, the phone left my palm as I followed the paramedics into our apartment and watched them flash a light in Paul's eyes.

"What happened tonight, sir?"

"I fell." Paul seemed to come to.

"Did you faint? Lose consciousness?"

"Lola. Raccoon."

"Lola?"

"Our dog," I blurted, behind them, wiping my nose on the sleeve of my pajamas. "She goes nuts when she sees raccoons. Normally, she's sedate. Squirrels, rats, raccoons. They ignite something in her. She—" I bit the inside of my lip. Who was this babbling idiot? Sedate? Ignite? How did those words even enter my head?

"It looks like your shoulder is dislocated, sir. I'm going to try and remove your jacket."

Paul shrieked when they attempted to release his arm.

"We'll leave it on, then. Can you stand up?"

Shakily, Paul tried to stand. On his uninjured side, the male paramedic gripped his armpit and helped him to his feet. "Do I have time to get dressed?" An inappropriate laugh flew though my lips.

"We're taking your husband to East General. He'll be in the ER."

"No!" The force of my voice shocked me. "Wait." No way was I going to let Paul get in that ambulance without me. Not when he looked like a lost little boy. While the paramedics gingerly helped my husband onto a stretcher, I grabbed a pair of pants and a sweater. In the bathroom, I yanked them on. Then I snatched sneakers from the closet and tugged a brush through my hair. Paul was already rolled down the hall by the time I was dressed; the paramedics were opening the outside door. On my way out, I pulled my raincoat off its hanger in the entryway closet and lifted my keys off the hook. To Lola, still penitent in the corner, still strapped to her leash, I commanded, "Stay." Not that it was necessary. I knew she wouldn't move.

Chapter Twenty-three

"You have no right!" a shirtless man screeched at a police officer as the gurney pushed through the ambulance bay doors into the emergency room. Blood smears bisected his chest. His beltless pants hung perilously low. "That's *my* property!" With bored looks on their faces, two NYPD officers restrained him with gloved hands. In a far corner, a toddler wailed snot down his face. Beside him, a woman with wild hair keened, "I'm not supposed to be here. I'm not supposed to be here."

I remembered the bleachy, barfy smell of a hospital, but not the madhouse sounds. The drumbeat of rain outside and the bug-zapper hiss of the flickering fluorescent lighting added a haunted-house vibe. Police radios crackled and phones trilled and people yelled and a distant siren sent a shrill cry into the night. Over the crazy din, a millennial doctor in brow-line glasses hollered, "On my count. One, two, three."

I took it all in with the odd sensation of standing next to myself. Paul yowled as he was transferred from the gurney to an examining table. A huge round lamp was positioned over his head. The doctor bent over his bloody forehead. She asked loudly, "Did you lose consciousness, sir?" Her mahogany hair, twisted into a claw clip, was as shiny as polished topaz.

"Raccoon." Paul's voice was tight.

The doctor turned to me. "Did he lose consciousness?"

"I don't know. He fell in the park. Our dog lunged at a raccoon. His shoulder is hurt. And his head."

It suddenly struck me that losing consciousness was the bad thing, since everyone asked about it. A wave of anger washed over me. "He's conscious now," I wanted to shout. "Fix him!" Couldn't they see the gash on his bloody forehead? His dangling arm? The crowd of nurses seemed excessive. All those moving hands and no one thought to clean the blood off his face? One nurse extricated Paul's good arm from his parka and cut the sleeve of his shirt with snub-nosed scissors; another swabbed the area and inserted a needle in his inner elbow. While the doctor listened to Paul's heartbeat through her stethoscope, someone in purple scrubs removed his shoes and socks and threw them on the floor. He pressed his gloved hands up and down Paul's legs. No one addressed the real problem. "It's his arm," I whimpered. "It hurts him."

"Can you tell me your name, sir?"

When Paul didn't answer, I said, "Judge Paul Agarra." His job title felt like an important addition. I wanted her to know he wasn't some guy off the street. He'd never stand shirtless in an ER and shout about unfairness. Judge Paul Agarra put people in prison for life. Stupidly, I added, "You're not going to cut off his jacket, are you? It's his favorite."

With a flat-line smile, the nurse at Paul's legs corralled me out of the examining area. He said, "It's best to wait over there," wherever "over there" was. He may have pointed, but it didn't register. I decided not to move. Who was he to know what was best for me? I was stunned when he promptly shut the curtain in my face.

With my raincoat still on and my purse pressed to my chest, I crept up to the crack in the curtain and watched. They must have given Paul a massive painkiller because he was silent and spongy when two males sat him up from behind while the doctor and another woman lowered his jacket. It was stained with blood. Would they drop that on the floor, too?

Could I throw a Patagonia parka in the wash with Oxi-Clean?

"Stay with us, Judge." The doctor rubbed her knuckles on Paul's chest. "Open your eyes," she commanded.

Stay with us? Fresh tears stung my eyes. Was Paul leaving us?

"There you go," she said to him. "Look at me." Paul obeyed, his eyes unfocused. His lower lip glistened with saliva. He looked the way Lola looked when we drugged her with acepromazine for a long car ride.

"Before we pop it back in, we need to rule out fracture." The doctor spoke quietly to a nurse, or maybe an intern. All were freakishly young. Or was I old? The last time I'd been in an emergency room was years ago with my mom. Dad found her passed out on the bathroom floor. She, too, had hit her head and was bleeding down her face. But the doctor who'd stitched her up was grandfatherly. Or did it seem that way because I was a kid? My body swayed. Mom was dead a few months after her day in the ER and she hadn't had anything popped back in.

Suddenly, the curtain swooshed open. I stood stricken, as though I'd been caught peering through the keyhole in a bathroom door. "I didn't mean to spy." The shiny-haired physician smiled gently and said, "I'm Dr. Mishra. The attending." Surprising me, she held out a bare hand. I shook it, though I didn't want to. Weren't emergency rooms petri dishes of drug-resistant superbugs?

"You are?" she asked.

"Fay. Paul's wife. Fay Agarra."

"Ah, good." She seemed relieved that I had marital authority, even though I had no business being a wife at all. Not when I'd pushed my husband into the rain and caused the whole damn mess. Dr. Mishra asked, "Can you tell me more about what happened?"

The moment I opened my mouth, tears exploded from my eyes. "It's my fault. He didn't want to go out. I made him. Our dog. She needs exercise. I think they were gone a long time. But I'm not sure. I had Pandora on. When Paul came home, his face was bloody and his arm was weird. Is his shoulder dislocated?"

"Yes. Though there may be a fracture, too. How old is he?"

"Sixty-eight."

"Is he on any medications?"

"Cholesterol pills."

"Any history of heart disease or stroke?"

"Is high cholesterol heart disease?"

"Not necessarily. Is Paul allergic to any medications?"

"I don't think so."

My nose ran mucus into the divot above my lip.

Without thinking, I swiped my germy hand over it. "Is something else cut?" I asked, sniffing. "The blood."

"A head contusion produces copious amounts of blood." She stepped over to the nurse's station and plucked two tissues from a box on the desk. As she handed them to me, she asked, "Does he take baby aspirin daily?"

"Yes."

"That would also explain the high bleed."

"Even his teeth were bloody."

"His teeth? He had blood in his mouth?"

"Yes. I think so. On his teeth."

"I'll take a closer look. He may have bitten his tongue."

"It's completely my fault." My voice quivered as I wept.

She reached up and squeezed my upper arm. That small gesture filled me with gratitude. I knew Paul was in good hands.

"I'll let you know more as soon as we look at the X-rays. Hopefully, he won't need surgery."

"Okay." I sniffed hard. "Thank you so much." The word "surgery" didn't sink in. I threw my arms around Dr. Mishra. She patted my back and extricated herself quickly. "There's a café in the basement," she said. "If you want coffee or anything."

"Roger that."

Roger that? I winced. Ever since I'd seen Paul's bloodied face through the window in our building's door, my mouth had a mind of its own.

An hour passed. Maybe two. Or maybe the whole night. Like a casino, there were no windows in the waiting room, no clock to inform a person if it was night or day. I ate pretzels from a vending machine. I'd brought my phone, but forgotten the charger. I used my last bar to text Isaac Lewis, Paul's court clerk. "Paul took a tumble in the park." My tone was breezy. I didn't want Isaac to worry. "Won't be in. More deets later. Xo."

At least, I think that's what I texted. I'd left my glasses on the bedside table at home. Magazine articles were a blur of celebrity faces and smudged headlines. *Who* was dancing with the stars?

I should have called Anita first. Or my brother Nathan, in California. Nate would have calmly told me what to do. Anita would have rushed down to sit with me. She would have remembered her charger and stopped by Starbucks to buy me a skim latte and protein box. She would call Paul's son for me, reassure him that all was in hand. Anita would know how to manage this. But I hadn't been able to think straight since Paul came home with his floppy arm. My brain was a jumble of self-recrimination and fear. If Paul had lost consciousness, what did that mean? Had he lain facedown on the wet walkway in the park while I'd danced around our apartment to *Disco Inferno*?

A slender man in turquoise scrubs had entered and exited the waiting area several times. He carried manila folders and walked with the clipped gait of authority. I leaped up from my seat before he had a chance to stride off once more. "Could you please find out what's taking so long with my husband's X-ray?"

"There was an accident on the FDR Drive," he said. "That may be it."

"Can I bring him a snack? Something from the café in the basement?"

Smiling blandly, he said, "I'm sure the doctor will be right out."

In a military turn, he rotated on his sneakers and left me. I sat back down. All I could think of were Paul's bare feet. His bent toes, the spider veins on his ankles, the yellowed skin on his heels. Lying there, shoeless, he'd looked so vulnerable. A nurse had given me a plastic bag with his clothes. The muddy shoes and bloody jacket weighed down the bottom of it, a heavy reminder that I'd made Paul walk Lola in the rain. Would they give him clean socks to wear home?

Would I have to dress him in his dirty clothes? The shirt with the cutoff arm?

"Mrs. Agarra?"

At last, Dr. Mishra appeared. She stood next to another female doctor. Older, rounder. More doctorly looking. Her ebony hair had streaks of bluish gray. Her dark eyes crinkled at the corners. I made a move to stand, but Dr. Mishra rested her hand on my shoulder and sat in the chair on my right. The other doctor sat to my left.

"This is the orthopedic surgeon, Dr. Kanton."

Orthopedic? I thought. *Had something happened to Paul's bare feet?*

"I know this has been a long night for you," Dr. Kanton said. I nodded even though I had no idea how many hours I'd been there. I entwined my arms in front of my chest. Suddenly, I noticed I'd forgotten to wear a bra. My breasts hung heavily beneath my sweater. Mortified, I quickly closed the flaps of my raincoat.

"Your husband has a serious proximal humerus fracture," the surgeon continued. "He's broken his shoulder."

I sucked in air.

"A surgical repair is definitely needed. It's a fairly straightforward procedure. We open the shoulder *here.*" She ran the edge of her hand down to her armpit. "First, we realign the fracture. Then we attach a metal plate to the arm bone to hold it in place while it heals."

I nodded as if I understood. As if I weren't feeling the weight of my bare breasts. I fastened an intelligent look on my face and let the doctor's words bounce off me.

". . . stands for open reduction internal fixation . . . titanium screws . . . sutures or surgical staples. . . ."

Nod, nod. Thoughtful look. I wished Paul were there with me, holding my hand and cooing, "Everything is going to be okay." I wanted the humming in my ears to stop.

". . . a full three months to heal . . . physical therapy after surgery. . . ."

Nod. Nod.

"His forehead?" I waited until Dr. Kanton's lips stopped moving. "Is it still bleeding?"

On my other side, Dr. Mishra leaned forward. "We were able to stitch it up," she said. "Skin is thin there. He won't have much of a scar."

"Ah. Good." *When had they done that? Wasn't he in X-ray?*

"I know this is a lot to take in, Mrs. Agarra," she said. "But Dr. Kanton is one of the best orthopedic surgeons in the city."

"Good. Good. Good."

"I'd like to operate first thing tomorrow morning."

When Dr. Kanton leaned toward me, two white coats brushed against my knees. Two stethoscopes dangled from two highly educated necks. The best in the city. She added, "Your husband is sedated right now. This type of fracture is extremely painful. I wouldn't want to put him through another day without fixing it."

"Fix it. Yes, definitely."

"So, why don't I take you in to see him? Then you can fill out some paperwork and I'll reserve the OR for tomorrow morning."

"Good, good. Yes. Please let me see him. I've been worried."

Dr. Mishra squeezed my hand. "This is a tough break. Literally. But we'll take good care of him."

Gratitude flushed my cheeks. Paul was going to be okay. He was in the hands of the best. After his surgery, when he was on the mend, I'd tell him how sorry I was. I'd make it up to him. During his months of recovery, I'd walk Lola for him, even in the snow. I'd never again goad him into taking her out when the weather was foul. I'd feed him fish tacos and roasted chicken thighs and rigatoni with garlic and oil. Baby arugula salad without the stems. All his favorites. I'd show him how good a wife could be.

"Take care," Dr. Mishra said, standing.

"You, too," I replied automatically. Then I stood and followed Dr. Kanton to see my husband.

Not once, not even for a second, did it occur to me to tell either doctor about Paul's cognitive weirdness, his shuffling gait, his personality change. All thoughts of difficulties understanding a menu, following the thread of a conversation, remembering his daughter-in-law's name, focusing in court, tumbling our lives into a carnival fun house, were elsewhere. The memory of Spain, and being left, never wormed its way into my consciousness. Only one thing mattered: my Paul, my man, my there kind of guy, was going to be repaired. He wasn't leaving me. He would come home. We would be *anded* again. Paul and Fay. Forever and ever. In sickness and in health.

Chapter Twenty-four

The room was dark. A hazy green aura from blipping lights cast slanted shadows across Paul's bed. He breathed heavily, sedated into a cavern of sleep, his mouth slack. A thick white bandage immobilized his arm and shoulder. A square of gauze was taped over the sutured cut on his forehead.

"Don't stay too long." Dr. Kanton rested a comforting hand on my back. "Paul's paperwork will be waiting for you downstairs at the admissions desk. After you sign everything, go home and get some rest. Paul won't be out of recovery before noon tomorrow."

"Okay." Pretty much all I said that night. Okay, nod, yes, good. I never thought to question anything. Certainly not anyone in a white coat with a stethoscope around her neck.

If only.

Following a soft squeeze of my shoulder, Dr. Kanton pivoted and left. Out of the corner of my eye, I saw the flip of her modest hem and the boxy heel of her sensible shoe. Trustworthy clothes.

"My love?"

Careful not to lean on anything that would shift his shoulder, I bent down to whisper in Paul's ear, "I'm here. Everything's going to be okay. One of the best surgeons in the city is going to fix your shoulder first thing in the morning."

If I could have, I would have crawled into bed with Paul and nestled into the downy warmth of his chest. I would have planted myself where I belonged. Instead, my hand drifted to the top of his head. I smoothed my husband's hair, inhaled his Paul smell.

"I'm sorry, I'm sorry, I'm sorry." Like the chugging of steel wheels on a rail, I repeated those two words over and over. "I'm sorry, I'm sorry." Then, these three: "I love you, I love you, I love you."

Paul's eyebrows pressed together. I took it as a sign that he recognized my voice. He knew he wasn't alone. "I'm right here. Everything is going to be okay."

That night, I absolutely believed it.

Worried that I might wake him up, I obeyed the doctor's orders and left. I summoned my last shred of energy to trudge down the dim hallway, still wearing my raincoat. My purse was still clutched to my braless breasts. The hospital quiet was unnerving. Dead silent. Even the nurses sat soundlessly beneath spills of soft light, notating files. Dotting the *i*'s and crossing the *t*'s. I pushed the elevator button with my knuckle. Had I ever washed my hands? My brain was packed in cotton. Alone in the elevator car, I leaned against the wall and felt the slow descent. On the first floor, I stepped out onto the shiny marble floor and followed the signs pointing to the admissions desk. Dr. Kanton was right. Paul's paperwork was waiting for me.

"I left my glasses at home," I laughed wearily.

"It's pretty standard stuff." The woman behind the desk had a kind face. Her cheeks were round and pink. She'd draped a pastel cardigan over her shoulders the way my mother always had. Fleetingly, I wondered if she was an insomniac. Who else would choose to work in the middle of the night? "Consent to surgery," she said, pointing to signature spaces on the form, "permission to bill your insurance, a listing of risks."

"Risks?"

She read: "All operations and procedures carry the risk of unsuccessful results, complications, injur—"

"Got it." Okay, nod, yes.

I signed on the blurry dotted line.

By the time I got home, night was close to day. Our apartment looked like we'd been abducted by aliens. Pandora's dance station still played on the TV, lights illuminated every room, the corner of my side of the bedding was triangled down. I set down my purse, peeled off my raincoat.

"Lola?"

The click of her toenails was tentative. She peered around the edge of our bed's footboard, her ears flat.

"Oh, baby," I said, softly. "It's okay. Come here."

For once, she came to me when I asked her to. Her leash—still attached—dragged behind her. That haughty tail of hers was curled into a comma between her legs. I sank onto the rug beside our bed and took her face in my hands. I kissed her nose. "Damn raccoon." Unlocking the harness across her chest, I slid it over her head and released her. I ran my hand over the velvety fur on her ears. I took her into my arms. Lola melted her muscular body into me, safe now.

From my position on the floor, I couldn't see the clock. But I knew it was late. Or early. Too late to text John in Boston. Too early to call Anita and tell her what had happened. Only one person I knew was sure to be up. On hands and knees, I crawled over to the bedside table, grabbed the landline, and scrolled though the contacts.

"Nathan?"

"Are you okay?" My brother's voice was raspy. Though it was three hours earlier in California, it was still late. He was smoking a cigarette, I could tell, and had been reading a novel about warlords or epic medieval intrigues or parallel universes populated by gynoids.

"Paul broke his shoulder." Crawling back to the rug, I sat with Lola. I ran my open palm down her back to soothe us both.

"Shit."

"He's in the hospital."

"Ach."

"I feel so . . . hospitals, you know."

"I know."

He did know. Hospitals were where our family members went to die. First, Mom. Then, while I was in college, our dad died after a car wreck, and later our brother, Joey, died after a heroin overdose. Both left us in a hospital that could do nothing but pronounce their official times of death. It had all been so embarrassingly clichéd. Dad was driving home from a bar and Joey was celebrating his release from rehab. More than once, Nathan had stabbed Joey's thigh with a naloxone pen, carted him to the emergency room, held the barf bowl while he detoxed, administered the antivirals he needed to control his hepatitis C. With our dad, Nathan was the next of kin called when our father's blackouts or bar brawls resulted in a broken nose or busted lip or split forehead. He knew all about the crazed yelling in a trauma center and the vomity scent of a hospital floor. He understood feeling utterly alone.

"So, what, surgery?"

"Yeah." I sighed.

"Crap."

As adults who'd lived through the loss of our family, Nathan and I spoke in shorthand. My brother didn't need to ask how I was doing. I didn't need to pretend I wasn't flattened by guilt and fear. We knew and loved each other in a way that was deeper than the ocean and wider than the sky.

"You're stronger than you think," he said, sucking in the first drag of a fresh cigarette. I'd long ago stopped begging him to quit. His scars, I knew, were excruciating. It's a myth that time heals everything.

"Promise?"

Nathan laughed. He blew the poison through his lips in a long *whooo*.

"I love you," I said.

"I know." I could hear the smile in his voice when I hung up.

Curled into each other, Lola and I fell asleep on the rug.

Chapter Twenty-five

"Should I come out?" John called me seconds after reading my morning text. "I mean, is it bad?"

"A broken shoulder is definitely bad," I said. "But there's nothing to do but wait until he's out of surgery."

"Who's the surgeon? I'll Google him."

"He's a she. Dr. Kanton."

I heard his fingers fly across the keyboard. "First name?"

Had she told me? "I don't know. She's the best in the city."

"They all say that," he said. "Which hospital?"

"East General."

"East General? Christ, Fay. Wouldn't Columbia Pres be a better choice? Mount Sinai?"

"I didn't have a choice. The paramedics took him there."

His sigh was loud and long. "Unless Dad was dying, you should have called Columbia directly. Or arranged for him to be moved as soon as he was stable."

"I called 911."

"Your first mistake."

I almost told John he was dead wrong. My first mistake was badgering his father to go out in the rain. So there.

"Look, John, it was an emergency. He'd hit his head, too. He was bleeding. I'm sure Dr. Kanton knows what she's doing. She explained the whole procedure to me."

He read, "'A stellar surgeon and person.'" In a pompous tone, he added, "She got four stars. A total of seven reviews."

What, he was looking her up on Yelp?

"In New York City, you can get a five-star surgeon. Who cares what type of person they are?"

My body was a tangle of aches from sleeping on the floor. Isaac had already left two messages. At sunrise, Lola had returned to her old self. More asleep than awake, I'd felt her get up and leave me. I'd heard her plop down in the safety of her crate. Her room. By the time I unfolded myself into the day, she was back to regarding me disdainfully.

"I have to get going," I told John. "To the hospital."

"You'll call, then."

"I'll call."

Anita Pritchard had an altogether different reaction: "I'm on my way."

Unable to move, I stood naked beneath the down rush of steaming water in the shower, my hair pasted to my forehead, my arms limp. The day had barely begun and I was already exhausted.

Anita buzzed from the vestibule while my hair was still damp. Lola barked her way up the stairs.

"Not today," I said, with a period. My genius dog understood. Clipping short her loud alert that someone was at the door, she made her way to the upstairs dog bed and nestled into its soft fleece.

True to form, Anita bustled into the apartment with a venti skim latte from Starbucks and an egg-and-cheese protein box. "I know you," she said. "You'll eat chips in the hospital cafeteria. You'll drink Diet Coke all day."

"Not *all* day," I replied. "And it was pretzels."

She set the food and coffee on the kitchen table and circled her arms around me. "He's not your mom. He's not your dad."

Tears rose up by degrees. First, I felt a pressing in my chest, then a tingling across my face, then slippage down my cheeks.

"Sit," Anita said. "Eat protein." I sat and ate protein and blew my nose while I told my best friend about the ordeal.

"Lola." Anita cocked one brow. Lola tilted her nose to the floor.

"It's not her fault," I said. "It's mine. Paul's been so—" I didn't tell her the truth, the whole truth, and nothing but. Instead, I said, "He's been so *selfish* lately. I wanted to punish him. I'm a horrible wife."

"You're not horrible, Fay. You're spiteful."

A chuckle burped through my lips.

"All wives are spiteful now and then." Anita snapped a detergent pod into the dishwasher dispenser. "So I hear."

As I swallowed the last bites of cheese, I heard the dishwasher rumble on and the water swish around. I watched Anita suds the soapstone countertop and wipe down the butcher-block table. The clean scent of dish soap swirled through the air. Turning to me, she asked, "Do you know when Paul will be out of surgery?"

"Noon. That's what the doctor said."

"Good. I have time to walk Lola while you get dressed."

Sometimes, I wanted to slide my hand into Anita's palm and beg her to hang on to me forever.

We sat. We waited. *The View* morphed into *The Chew.* Noon edged up to one o'clock, then neared two. The coffeemaker in the corner of the surgical waiting room was broken. Anita slyly checked the time on her phone. "A text from my mom," she lied. Then she said, "Be right back," and stood up and marched over to the reception desk.

It felt peaceful in limbo. I didn't mind watching Mario Batali make something cheesy in his orange Crocs and cargo shorts. The longer we waited, the less real it felt. We were picking Paul up. Plain and simple. We were waiting for him to get dressed. The three of us would have lunch. Was there a good pizza place nearby?

"Fay?"

Looking up, I was startled to see Paul's law clerk.

Isaac's physique filled the room. Not at all fat, he was nonetheless huge. His shoulders could carry an ox yoke. When a person looked at Isaac Lewis, they could see that he was the sort of man who would—and could—carry them out of a collapsed building.

"John called me," he said. "How's the judge?"

"Still in surgery."

In Isaac's alarmed expression, I suddenly realized how long Anita and I had been sitting there. "You're worried about his trial?" I asked, stupidly.

"I arranged for a backup judge."

"Ah. Good. I think he may need, um, a few more days."

Anita reappeared. "Isaac!" She kissed his cheek. "Do you know something we don't know? Reception won't tell me anything."

He said, "No," but his eyes flicked to the right. A sign, Paul once told me, of lying. "Defendants think they are so smart," he'd said. "Lies are always written on a face."

"I'm going to get food," Anita announced. Then she turned toward the elevator. "If you see Paul before I get back, Fay, give him a kiss from me. On the lips."

I laughed. Isaac settled in the chair next to me and took my hand. Leaning close, he said, "Paul's surgery may be a blessing."

I made a face.

"Not a *blessing*," he rushed in. "Wrong word. It's just that, well, remember what we talked about?"

"His new medication?"

"Yeah." He knew I was covering up. I knew that he knew. "Since then," he said in a low voice, "things have slipped a little, to be honest. Paul has had trouble understanding briefs. Lately, he's been asking questions in court that show he's not listening. Or, maybe he's listening, but not fully comprehending. It seems to come and go. I've been planning to talk to him about retirement. You know, soon. I'm not sure how much more I can cover for him. Or how much I should."

"I see," I said, not sure what else to say.

"A long recovery may be just what he needs to ease himself off the bench. No shame. Not like saying he's leaving to spend more time with family. No one ever believes that. I'm thinking, maybe we have a silver lining here? You know, not as bad as a competency hearing."

My heart thudded. Competency hearing? Had things gotten that bad?

"Mrs. Agarra?"

At last, the surgeon stepped through the door. I leaped up. Still dressed in green scrubs, she said, "Sit. Please. We met in the emergency room. I'm Dr. Kanton."

I sat. I introduced Isaac. I asked, "Is Paul okay?"

Pausing ever so slightly, Dr. Kanton said, "Yes."

My heart dropped to my knees. A pause.

"He's still in recovery," she said, sitting next to me with her elbows on her knees and her fingers braided. "As you know, it was a severe break, made more complicated by osteoarthritis in the acromioclavicular joint."

Nodding, I said, "Ah," even as I wondered, *Had I known his break was severe? The night before, wasn't it only* serious?

"I was able to repair the humerus fracture and secure the titanium plates," the surgeon continued. "The fracture tore a nerve, making the repair somewhat tricky. Paul was under general anesthesia longer than I'd like, but he'll come out of it soon."

"He's still asleep?"

"No. He's awake. In the recovery room. As I said." Her clipped sentences felt slightly punitive. My cheeks flushed. I realigned my features to look more mature. Since Paul's accident, I'd felt as though my adulthood had slithered away. Seeped through the floorboards. In its place was the child I remembered: a teenage kid who promised God she would give up MTV and anything else He wanted if He would erase the hollow stare in her mother's eyes.

"Anesthesia can linger in the body," said Dr. Kanton. "It can take time to clear a patient's disorientation."

"I see." Of course, I didn't see at all. I cocked my head pensively.

"When can we go in?" Isaac asked.

"One visitor for now. Family." She stood, and I did, too. Leaving Isaac in the waiting room, I followed Dr. Kanton like a puppy. On our way down the hall, she turned to me and said, "Don't be alarmed if your husband seems dazed. He's on oxygen. To help his body recover as fast as possible."

"I see."

Of course, I didn't see anything at all.

"Judge?" The surgeon's loud voice was jarring in the quiet around Paul's bed. "You're in the recovery room. You had surgery to fix your broken shoulder. Your wife is here to see you. It's time to wake up."

My husband slowly opened his eyes.

"Paul?" Tears rained down my cheeks.

Propped up on a pillow, his shoulder and arm encased in a surgical sling, Paul stared blankly. His nose and mouth were covered by an oxygen mask. With each breath, it fogged up.

"I'm here, my love."

Pulling a penlight from her breast pocket, Dr. Kanton clicked it on and flicked it in Paul's eyes. "Paul?"

From deep within his throat, a garbled noise tumbled into the oxygen mask. "*Hoam. Git owa.*"

I glanced at Dr. Kanton. When she nodded, I lifted the oxygen mask off his face. "Say that again?"

"Get me out of here."

It was muddled, but clear enough to understand. The doctor said, "That's a good sign."

"It is?"

"He's coming around."

"Shhhh," Paul whispered. "What's that noise?"

Dr. Kanton pushed some button on the beeping machine at the foot of Paul's bed and said to me, "Keep that oxygen flowing."

I returned Paul's mask to his nose and mouth. I smoothed the wiry hair on top of his head. Despite the muffle of the mask, I heard him say, "They're just outside the door."

"Who?"

"Paul. You're safe." Again, Dr. Kanton raised the decibel level of her voice as if to penetrate his fog. "You are in a hospital. Your wife is here. Can you tell me what year this is?"

Paul twisted his neck left and right. "*Mmgaah.*"

"Paul? Judge?" Dr. Kanton was shouting again. "I told you where you are. Can you tell me what I said?"

He looked at her like she was insane.

Paul's free hand flailed in the direction of the IV line running into his vein. He tried to grasp it. Or was he reaching for my hand? I sandwiched his palm between both of mine and squeezed.

"What month is this? What season?" Dr. Kanton continued yelling questions. "Do you know what city you live in?"

Again, Paul stretched his neck and made a noise. "It sounds like he's in pain," I said. "Is he in pain?"

"Discomfort and paranoia are not uncommon." To Paul, she asked, "Do you recognize your wife?"

Paul stared blankly. The blood left my face.

"What's happened?"

Ignoring me, Dr. Kanton pointed to her watch. "Can you tell me what this is, Paul? This?" She held up a pen. He said nothing.

"What's wrong with my husband?"

The surgeon's lips were pressed into a white line. She looped around the foot of Paul's bed and rested her hand on my upper arm. "I need you to calm down."

"Calm down? His surgery was hours ago. You said he was fine."

"I said that anesthesia can have aftereffects. Especially in the elderly."

Elderly? She was talking about my Paul. Judge Paul Agarra.

"What does he need?" I asked. "More oxygen? Protein?"

"Give it a few days." She returned the penlight to her pocket and moved closer to the door.

"Days? Of what?"

"Rest. Sometimes, cognitive fog lasts longer than we'd like."

I stared at her. "What are you talking about?"

"Mrs. Agarra." She smiled fakely. "The best course of action is to reassess in a day or two." She seemed put out, as if Paul hadn't played by the rules. As if I was being pushy. Before she left, she said, "Get some rest yourself, okay?" In a flash of green scrubs, she was gone.

I stood there, dumbfounded. Get some rest? *What?*

In a conspiratorial whisper, Paul murmured beneath his mask, "She's gone. Help me up."

Chapter Twenty-six

When Paul was moved into a regular room, I should have made a fuss. "He's not recovered," I should have said. "Why did he leave the recovery room?" Instead, I stood at my husband's bedside and picked up where Dr. Kanton left off. "You're in the hospital, Paul. You broke your shoulder. Can you tell me what I just said?"

Paul stared blindly at the ceiling. His oxygen mask was gone. He opened his mouth and mumbled, "Did you ask me?" In flashes of recognition, I could see that he knew me. Just as abruptly, I could see that he didn't. My brain couldn't process everything. It felt encased in Bubble Wrap. Apart from reality. Protected against a hard landing.

Utterly exhausted, I slumped in the chair next to Paul's bed and stared at the *drip, drip* of his IV.

By then, Anita had left, as had Isaac. It was late afternoon. Maybe the middle of the night? All of a sudden, I became aware of a nauseating smell.

"Oh," I said.

"We got here as soon as we could." Kate Agarra deposited a huge bouquet of flowers in my arms. The cloying aroma sickened me. "Beautiful," I said, breathing through my mouth. "I'll see if the nurse has a vase."

"Forget about that," John commanded. "Where is the doctor?"

"Dad?" Kate positioned herself in front of Paul's face. As if he were blind, for God's sake. She wore lululemon joggers and running shoes. "We're here for you. Edie sends her love. She couldn't leave her tutoring session. But, like I said, we're here."

Had she gone straight from the gym to the airport?

"Why isn't Dad in a private room?"

I looked at John and blinked. I had no idea why Paul was in a shared room. It's where they put him. After they removed him from the recovery room when he wasn't recovered at all.

"What's the woman's name?" My stepson fired questions at me.

"What woman?" I didn't appreciate his tone.

Paul swatted his free hand in front of his face. The other one was tucked into a surgical sling. He asked Kate, "Do I know you?"

"The surgeon," John said, impatiently. "What's her name again?"

"Dr. Kanton."

"First name?"

Still, I didn't know. Did I need to know? What difference did it make?

"They know who she is at the nurses' station."

With my arms puking flowers, I watched John stomp down the hall in full asshole mode. His sense of entitlement oozed from his pores. His iPhone, of course, was in his hand. It looked vaguely threatening, as if he had an attorney on speed dial.

"Page Dr. Kanton for me," I heard him say.

"You are?"

Instantly, that nurse became my favorite.

"John Agarra. A-G-A-R-R-A. Son of Judge Paul Agarra."

"Need anything? Juice? A bagel?" Leaving Kate cooing into Paul's face, I left to find a vase. Outside Paul's room, a strong urge to run overtook me. The elevator was so, so close. A teenage volunteer skipped up to me and inserted her face into the blossoms in my arms. "Gorgeous."

"My husband hates cut flowers," I said. "They represent death to him. The beginning of decay."

The girl stared, her lips glistening. Sweetening my voice, I asked, "Do you happen to have something to put these in?"

With a nod, she plucked the monstrous bouquet from my hands and disappeared down the hall. The stink stayed on my clothes, my hands, my face. I made my way to the restroom and shut myself in a stall.

"Pull yourself together, Fay," I muttered. Then I did something I would never normally do: I sat on the toilet with my head in my hands. "You are a capable adult. You can handle this." I reminded myself to breathe in. Then, I reminded myself to breathe out. Repeat. I closed my eyes and pictured a glassine lake. I listened to my heart beating. *Ba blop. Ba blop.* I waited for my brain to rejoin my body. As soon as I felt sturdy enough to cope, I stood and unlocked the door. Marching to the sink, I splashed water on my face, not caring if my mascara ran or not. Had I even applied mascara that morning?

Dr. Kanton was back in Paul's room, flicking her little flashlight in his eyes and shouting again. "Can you tell me where you are, Judge?" He blinked at her disinterestedly. I stepped back. John stepped forward.

"What I need from you is a timetable," he informed

the doctor. His arms were crossed over his chest and his stance was wide. Kate straightened the mini Kleenex box next to Paul's beige pitcher of water.

The surgeon returned the penlight to her breast pocket. She inhaled and said, "Hmm." For the first time, I noticed that she was once a pretty woman. Her dark hair had been naturally black; the bluish undertone in her skin had been the ideal backdrop for sterling silver. I wondered, *Had she been muscled in medical school? Or had she always had soft edges?*

"Let's step outside."

Paul grunted when the three of us followed Dr. Kanton out of his room. A nursing assistant with a bathing bin passed us on his way in.

"Thank you." Kate gratefully squeezed the assistant's arm. He smiled. Kate Agarra was the type of wife who would learn all the nurses' names if her husband was in the hospital. She would show up with homemade cookies and T-shirts that read Team John. She'd cover John's bed with a quilt from home. A framed photo of Edie would stand in his sight line. Kate would never lie that her husband disliked flowers when it was really her problem. She wasn't the kind of woman who thought stale flower water smelled like rotting corpses.

"Yes, thank you!" I yelped to the assistant who was already at work in Paul's room.

Beyond my husband's earshot, Dr. Kanton began, "As I already explained to Mrs. Agarra, it's not uncommon for older patients to experience cognitive fog following surgery. The medical term is postoperative cognitive dysfunction, or POCD. It can last for days or weeks. According to one study, twelve percent of patients over sixty experience cognitive impairment for a full three months after surgery. Some even longer."

"Three months?" Stunned, John turned to me. "Did you know this?"

"I was told. As she said." *POC . . . what?*

"It's usually transient," Dr. Kanton said.

"Usually?" John gaped at her. "My father is a sitting judge."

"Yes. I am aware of that. Give it a chance to clear." Ever so slightly, her body turned toward the elevator. "The only time I've seen POCD descend into a permanent state is when the patient had cognitive impairment *before* surgery."

"What?" I swallowed dry spit. The airy bull pen seemed to suddenly lose its oxygen. I opened and closed my mouth like a cowfish on the beach. It wasn't obvious, but Dr. Kanton's shoulders ticked back to us. She asked me, "Did you ever notice any memory lapses or personality changes in your husband, Mrs. Agarra?"

"Like what?" Suddenly, I felt sick.

"Forgetting names more than usual, an inability to process or recall information, poor judgment, gait disturbances, that sort of thing."

"Fay?" John's voice was an ice pick.

"What do you mean by *permanent*?" I swiveled away from John and his self-righteous face.

Concern creased Dr. Kanton's forehead. "Well, we don't like to use the word 'dementia,' but there have been cases where patients develop symptoms similar to Alzheimer's disease."

I sucked in a sharp breath. She didn't want to use the word "dementia" yet she tossed out the *A* bomb?

"Getting lost in familiar places, severe memory and comprehension deficits, inappropriate behavior, language difficulty, blank stares, shuffling gait." All of a sudden, she was a talking textbook, rattling off a litany of everyone's worst nightmare. "Eventually, of course," she said, with no affect whatsoever, "these patients are unable to care for themselves."

My fingers, I noticed, were covering my lips. Kate piped up, "That's not Paul. My goodness, he's a judge."

"Fay?" John's voice jabbed at my eardrum again.

With a *conk*, the elevator doors opened.

"Dr. Fletcher?" Paul's internist ambled off. I should have known he'd have a peacock strut. "How did you—?"

"I called him." Emerging from the stairwell, gasping for air, was Brenda. Paul's ex. She gripped a large potted plant. Between gulps of air, she bellowed, "Did no one . . . else feel . . . the frightening aura . . . in that elevator?"

Kate lunged forward. "Let me take that for you, Mom." She lifted the spiky palm from her mother-in-law's arms and carted it into Paul's room.

"Southeast corner," Brenda called after her. "Feng shui."

Swiping her too-long hair off her sweaty face, Brenda planted a kiss on Dr. Fletcher's cheek. "Hi, Richard." Then she hugged her son and coolly said, "Hello, Fay," to me. My hand slithered down to my throat.

"Thank you for coming so quickly, Mom," John said. "You, too, Dr. Fletcher." He pressed both of his palms together in front of his chest, prayer-style. I wanted to slap the holier-than-thou look off his face.

With her outfit in full view, I saw that Brenda wore flowy pajama pants and a gauzy oversized shirt. Despite the damp weather. Not at all generously, I said, "I'm so sorry John got you out of bed." Then I added, "Everything is under control here."

"Under control?" John's nostrils flared into two white lines.

Dr. Fletcher extended his hand to Dr. Kanton. "I'm

Paul's primary," he said. "Richard Fletcher. Is there a complication?"

Turning his back on them, John faced me. "Did Isaac ever say anything to you?" I'd heard that same accusatory tone in Paul's courtroom. *Did you, or did you not, use your key to open the victim's door that night?*

"About what?" I said.

"Fay."

I turned on him. "I told you that your father was acting weird. Remember when he forgot Kate's award dinner? I said I was worried."

"That dinner was no big deal." Kate rejoined the group. She looked like she might cry. "A fund-raiser, really. I didn't mind that Paul forgot. Honestly."

"You said it was Paul's age, my fears." I felt my face getting hot. "You dismissed it." Pointing my flushed cheeks in Dr. Fletcher's direction, I felt anger rise into my chest. "Remember when I came to see you? I told you something was wrong with Paul. You practically shoved me out of your office. You referred *me* to a therapist. Like it was all in my head."

John glared. "You should have talked to Dad, not his doctor."

Now, my nostrils flared. "I did. He wouldn't listen. No one would."

"You should have *made* us listen to you."

What a joke. "Can anyone *make* any of you listen?"

"She has a point," Brenda said. "About Paul, I mean."

"Let's not get ahead of ourselves." Dr. Kanton held up her hands.

"Paul will be fine." Kate had gone white-eyed. "No need to get upset. He needs a few more days. Like the doctor said. Another week. Or month. That's all. Right?"

"I'm familiar with cognition issues following *cardiac* surgery," said Dr. Fletcher. "It's well documented in the literature. Though it's always difficult to pinpoint exact cause and effect in any case like this."

In his scholarly tone, I could hear him trying to cover his ass.

"Risk factors for all postsurgical neuropsychological deficits include age and preexisting impairment," Dr. Kanton added.

"Can we please speak English?" Brenda was practicing therapeutic breathing all over me. Her bulbous bosom ascended, perched midair, then dropped. I sidestepped out of her spitty exhalations.

"Did you ask her?"

Kate's fluttery hands lit on her husband's arm. "John."

"Surely, Dr. Kanton, you asked about my father's mental state before putting him under general anesthesia. Didn't you? You know, because he was sixty-seven."

"Is," I said, tightly. "And he's sixty-eight."

At the same time Dr. Kanton calmly said, "Mr. Agarra," Dr. Fletcher calmly said, "John." But neither could stop the freight train.

"Did you or didn't you?"

"I know this is a distressing time," she said.

"Distressing? I'd say this is more like a malpractice time."

"He's tired." Kate pursed her lips.

"All I want is a simple answer to a simple question." The muscles in John's jaw bulged in and out like a frog's gullet. "Did you ask my father's wife if she had noticed any cognitive changes in my dad?"

As I always did when John called me his father's wife, instead of Fay, I bristled. Dr. Kanton maintained a placid expression. It struck me that this very scene was probably role-played in medical school. Surely, surgeons faced angry, grief-stricken family members every day. Medical school wasn't only about anatomy and biology, was it? Doctors must be trained in the skill of maintaining composure while a family vented all over them. Weren't they? I wondered if Dr. Kanton was silently hoping John would lose steam in time for her next surgery.

"Your father had a severe proximal humerus fracture," she said in a measured way. "Surgery was his only option. At any age."

"You're not answering my question."

"John." Now I stepped in.

"It's okay, Mrs. Agarra. I know this situation is worrying for everyone." She faced Paul's son squarely. "All the necessary consent forms were signed. The risks were clearly written."

My face went pale. Curtly, John asked, "It that true, Fay? Did you read about the risk of dementia?"

"Again, we don't like to use that word," Dr. Kanton said.

"There was no choice, John," I said. "Your dad was badly hurt."

"Why won't anyone answer simple questions?" Now he was yelling. I wanted to smack him. How had Paul raised such a brat?

"Yes, John. I read the risks. I knew what might happen. There wasn't any choice."

I decided not to tell him that I'd forgotten my glasses that night, as well as my bra. I didn't tell him that I'd been so consumed by guilt and fear I could barely remember my own name. That white coats intimidated me. That hospitals only reminded me how limited medicine really was. People were poisoned by chemotherapy there. They died there, no matter what doctors and surgeons did. Daughters were left without mothers. Sisters lost brothers. Dads left without saying goodbye. I wanted to tell my stepson that he didn't have to yell at me. I already knew it was my fault. I was a spiteful wife and an inferior adult and I never should have been left in charge of another person's life.

"Sorry it took so long." The eager young volunteer with the cloud of flowers suddenly appeared. "I had to go to another floor to find a vase this big!"

No one said a word. We momentarily froze in place. Then, Dr. Kanton patted my shoulder and peeled away, with Dr. Fletcher on her heels. John and I stood with our pulses pushing out from our necks. Brenda continued her overdramatic breathing, now swooping both arms in the air on each inhale. With a stricken expression, the hospital volunteer scurried into Paul's room with the flowers.

"Southeast corner!" Brenda hollered after her.

Through gritted teeth, John announced, "I need caffeine." His mother asked, "Does the cafeteria have green tea?"

They left. Kate followed her husband to the elevator bank. Pajama-clad Brenda bustled behind them fretting, "If that elevator's energy is still black, I'll have to take the stairs."

With terror shooting through my veins, I scuffed into my husband's hospital room, past his roommate who watched *Dr. Phil* on his TV. Paul was asleep. The rhythmic snuffle of his snoring joined the beeping of the heart monitor. A geriatric symphony. I took his hand and lifted it to my lips. My kisses made little noises on each fingertip. *Pop, pop, pop.* I pressed his hand over my heart. He didn't wake up. Lowering myself into the chair next to Paul's head, I sat beside the potted palm and watched the flowers begin to die.

Dear God, what had I done?

Chapter Twenty-seven

I'd begun packing a lunch and eating it in the park with Lola. Not the park *proper*, where neighbors knew me and asked about Paul with downturned faces, but the shard of green between Hudson Crescent and Riverside Drive. Within its grassy borders, six curved benches encircled a sedate monument to honor military women. On a stone bench that was often damp and sometimes mossy, I sat and ate turkey sandwiches on sourdough and stared at your gleaming front door. I waited for the pediatrician to reappear. It had been months since destiny brought us together. That is, since I'd first seen him walking through the lobby we would one day call "ours." Surely he wondered what had happened to me?

"Good girl."

Lola didn't move when a Chihuahua mix scampered

past us. Clearly, those dogs will have sex with anything. Though her hackles spiked up, my girl didn't lunge. Nonetheless, I gripped her harness with one hand. Just in case. Then I bent down to run my thumb along the silk of her ears. She shot a tetchy glance at me. Outside, Lola wanted nothing to do with affection. Passing dogs might think she'd gone soft.

While I watched your door, I got to know my future neighbors. "Beats" began her park run on your granite steps, securing her wireless earphones and tucking her cell into an inner pocket of her sports leggings. "Goldman Sachs" met his idling town car at the curb in slate gray suits and pink ties. "Cowgirl" was a dog walker with a model's body who picked up and delivered purebreds. On hot days and cold, she wore Ugg boots and a curly-rimmed cowboy hat over her long blond hair. Whenever she passed Lola, she flicked a knowing glance at Lola's long, slender legs. They were both members of that rarefied club.

I also saw "Benny's Mommy." She was the elderly woman I'd met when I first sat in your stunning lobby, on your antique bench, and listened to her Pomeranian bark until he was hoarse. Each time I saw her—and her yippy powder puff—my heart lurched because I'd first seen Blake, the pediatrician, when I first saw her. Back then, I regularly wore my Hamptons outfit to the park in case I ran into him. Once or twice a skirt, if I'd shaved my legs.

In those heady days of anticipation—when I was sure I'd bump into Blake around every corner—I spent twenty minutes at the magnified mirror applying sunscreen, foundation, brow pencil, shadow, mascara, blush, lipstick—blotted once, then reapplied. I packed only tidy fruits for lunch: apples, bananas, dried apricots. Nothing drippy or sticky. I avoided salads, especially spinach, which tended to deposit green flecks in my teeth. I ate nothing with poppy seeds, ever. With my back straight and my ankles crossed elegantly beneath the bench, I sat in the parklet across the street from you waiting for my life to change.

Eventually, the tableau I'd created withered like lilies after Memorial Day. Who had time for so much self-care? Plus, didn't frequent showers strip the moisture from your skin? Why do laundry every week when Africans were thirsty? I mean, how selfish is that? Haircuts were expensive; color was ridiculous. Possibly carcinogenic! Removing mascara nightly was a pain. All that rubbing was probably ripping my eyelashes out. Why wear it at all? And my eyebrows? Well, I happened to see a headline on a beauty magazine in the subway: "Unruly Rules!" Seems a wild hedge over your eyes was *in*. Last time I took Paul to the doctor,

I noticed that a makeup ad at the bus stop featured a model who practically had a unibrow.

My sunscreen ritual was all that remained from my beauty regimen. Rain or shine or snow. Though I suspected it was a scam. My hands—slathered in sunscreen daily—were as freckled as Lola's long legs.

By the time the weather warmed again, I'd fallen back into a slipshod style: pulling on whatever I'd left on the chair or the floor the night before. Obviously, the pediatrician was in Yemen helping those poor babies. Or maybe in Turkey vaccinating refugees?

Then, one slightly cool day, I saw him.

I almost missed him entirely. He sat on an opposite bench, behind the monument in the little park across from your door. Had Lola not pulled me over to the grass so she could poop, I never would have circled around in search of a trash can for her laden baggie. Had the clementine sun not illuminated the reddish-gray curls that swirled above his open newspaper, I never would have been lured to look his way. Had fate itself not been in play, our paths would not have crossed again. But there he was. My savior.

He sat alone. No wedding ring. My chest was on fire.

"My apologies," I said, as sweetly as Scarlett O'Hara herself. I do declare, my voice lilted the tiniest bit. The pediatrician lifted his head and regarded me with a quizzical look. "There's no other dustbin," I said, accidentally slipping into Britspeak.

"Ah." He nodded and returned to reading his paper. I cursed myself for showing him how unattractive a person could look. I cringed at the stink of Lola's load. How could I breach park etiquette by depositing a full poop baggie in a trash receptacle near an occupied bench? Unless, of course, it was the long stretch of grass opposite the crab apple grove inside Riverside Park. The section with only *one* trash can at the very end of it. What, they expected us to carry the dangling baggie all the way to Hippo Playground?

After Blake and I were married, I'd devote myself to volunteering around the neighborhood. After I secured more trash cans, I'd tackle the thornier problem of stopping people from dumping stale bread to feed the "birds." Didn't they know they were only fattening brown rats that can produce as many as two thousand descendants a year?

With an apologetic giggle, I dropped the swaying baggie into the only available receptacle and backed away, sensing that the pediatrician, my Blake, preferred women without childbearing hips even when they'd never used them for that specific purpose. When I got home, I told myself, I'd regroup. I'd rev up my resolve to do daily squats. Before it was too late. Along with pelvic-floor contractions so I wouldn't feel like I had to pee all the time. I'd prepare for my new life as a doctor's wife.

A bus galumphed down Riverside Drive. I used the distraction to settle myself and Lola on a bench closer to the pediatrician. Surreptitiously, I blew into my palm to check my breath. With a life in free fall, how can a person remember to floss? I sat up straight and tucked my sneakers beneath the bench in a finishing school sort of way. I smoothed my hair and bit color into my lips. I sucked in my stomach. Then, I waited for the pediatrician to curl down the corner of his newspaper, drink me in, cock an eyebrow and ask, "Don't I know you?"

He licked his thumb and turned the newspaper page. I winced. After we were engaged, I'd lovingly remind him that there were more germs on an unwashed finger than there were on a toilet seat.

"Hmm. Do you?"

In my head, I practiced. Once he spotted me, I'd be coy. I'd flick my hair. I'd smile, but not overly so. No visible teeth. Not yet.

On that bench, beneath the leafy trees, I sat with a whimsical look. I waited for the pediatrician to say, "Seriously, I know you from somewhere."

"Hmm. Do you?"

"I do." I'd blush at how easily those two words danced off his tongue.

With a throaty chuckle, I'd chirp, "Of course you know me, silly. We're neighbors. I walk my dog here every day."

No. Lose the chirp. Too earnest.

"I live in a brownstone a few blocks away."

Better. Nicely vague. He needn't know that I didn't own the whole building. Not that my outfit made that likely. Dispassionately, I'd add, "I'm looking to relocate," allowing him the freedom to brag about you—his beautiful building—and invite me over for a drink and an unobstructed view of the river. One floor below the penthouse.

Quietly, I sat. Waiting. Breathing shallowly to keep my muffin top from spilling farther over my waistband.

Admittedly, I was unsettled to see the pediatrician reading the *New York Post.* It ran "health" pieces like the one about a man who had his penis cut off after it got stuck in a bottle. Instead of simply *breaking* the bottle and releasing himself, he left it attached for four days until his penis died of necrosis. The only reason I saw the story at all was because Anita e-mailed it to me under the subject line, "Necessary birth control." She doesn't have kids, either, only her childlessness is by choice.

Unlike the *New York Times,* my morning obsession, the *Post* ran daily horoscopes and celebrity gossip. Its cover headlines were quips in giant type, like "Putin on the Pressure" about our problems with Russia or "You May Now Cuss the Bride" about a brawl at a lavish wedding. Perhaps the pediatrician was researching a cure for attention deficit disorder? Maybe he read every newspaper in the city every day to avoid living in an elitist bubble. I swiveled my neck and *smized* in his direction. I smiled with my eyes. I let him know I wasn't one to judge. Often, I watched *BBC World News America* for an alternative point of view.

The pediatrician didn't look up. He licked his thumb again and turned another page. After swallowing a wave of disgust, I felt a flush of pride that my future husband was a speed reader. I pictured the stack of nonfiction hardcovers on his bedside table that he devoured nightly while propped up on goose-down pillows in his king-sized bed with a Duxiana mattress. The expensive mattress would be a thank-you gift from Doctors Without Borders. One he initially refused to accept. Though finally, humbly, with his hands pressed together Namaste-style, he'd tear up at their thoughtfulness. His tireless work in Syria *had* strained his back.

With a lingering sideways glance, I took in the pediatrician's outfit. It was similar to the one I'd seen in your lobby a while ago, the home we would one day share. Really, did a person need shirts in any color other than white? When you owned suede brogues, did you need another pair of shoes? Oh, wait. Upon a closer look, I saw that his shoes were *Wallabees*, those boxy suede shoes from the seventies. My heart fluttered. How adorably *him*. My Blake was no slave to fashion. There would be gobs of space in his (probably walk-in) closet.

He turned another page. Then another. Thumb, lick, grip page, turn. Look at my man go! Suddenly, in a move that a gazelle would envy, the pediatrician was up and striding toward Hudson Crescent. He walked straight for your front door. The very entrance we would pass through as husband and wife, though I wouldn't expect him to carry me across the threshold. Unless he insisted. And wore a back brace. His exit was so unexpected, so riveting to watch, I missed the chance to seductively say, "Bye-bye." He left his newspaper folded on the bench. Clearly, the pediatrician's method of recycling was to leave reading material for someone less fortunate. Why else would he have folded it? Generosity like that didn't come along every day.

"Ready for a walk in the park?" I asked Lola, my voice aflutter.

We both stood and stretched and crossed the Drive to the long patch of grass opposite the crab apple grove, grinning like puppies.

Chapter Twenty-eight

When she walked fast, which was her only speed, her high ponytail swung like a metronome. She mentioned her name, I think. I liked her ballet flats. I may, or may not, have told her that. A solitaire diamond sparkled on her ring finger. Its setting struck me as too old-fashioned for a fresh-faced young woman. Probably belonged to her fiancé's grandmother.

"I'm here to help you plan what's next," she said. Paul was awake, but only vaguely alert. John and Kate were back in Boston; Brenda was oming somewhere. Isaac and Anita were both at work. I was alone in the quiet.

"I'm sorry. Who are you again?"

She may have asked me to leave the chair next to Paul's bed and follow her to a cubicle behind the nurses' station. Maybe I just followed her numbly. I know we both sat down, knee to knee. Leaning forward, the young woman pressed her smooth hand on top of mine and said, "I'm Nicole. A social worker. No need to apologize. It's common for caretakers to feel fuzzy. That's completely normal. This is certainly an over-whelming time."

The only word I processed was "caretaker." Is that who I was now? Was I no longer Paul's wife?

A closed manila folder sat on Nicole's flat lap. Its label was printed with our last name: Agarra. She said, "I have a list for you."

"List. Okay. Got it." The air smelled like chili. Had someone brought in lunch? Dinner?

"Paul will need intensive aftercare," she said.

"Physical therapy."

"Among other things." She opened the folder. "You live on the Upper West Side, right?"

"Right."

"Let's find options in your neighborhood."

"Yes. Let's." Suddenly, I wondered if I'd remem-bered to feed Lola that morning. Had I left the glass backyard exit open? Could she get to the doggie door? I flicked my head in an effort to break my brain free from its cushioned shell. How long would *my* cognitive impairment last?

"Eighty-Sixth and West End, Eighty-Eighth and

Riverside Drive, Columbus near Ninety-Sixth." Nicole rattled off addresses.

"Uh-huh."

"Seems the average cost is about sixteen."

"Sixteen?"

"Thousand."

"A year?"

"A month."

My jaw went slack. "Sixteen thousand dollars a month for rehab?"

"Well—" She lifted her lips in a half smile. Had she practiced that look in a mirror? "We're actually talking about skilled nursing care. In-patient facilities."

I stared. Not comprehending.

"In a nursing home, they will care for your husband around the clock and help him restore as much function as possible."

"Nursing home? What are you talking about?"

In slow motion, Nicole closed the yellow folder on her lap. "Mrs. Agarra, I know this is hard to hear. But your husband may not regain full cognitive function. We need to prepare ourselves for what may come."

A headache had started that morning. Earlier, I'd felt it creep toward my temple, my eyeball. Now, it squeezed the entire side of my face.

"Like what?" I asked, even as I didn't remotely want to know.

"Needing assistance with dressing, bathing, meals. Wandering, forgetting your home address and phone number. Not knowing the time of day or night, incontinence, loss of bowel control, inability to speak full sentences or at all. Some patients develop delusions, hallucinations, compulsions like hoarding or hand washing. Often, it's worse at night, a symptom called 'sundowning.' In its latest stage, patients with severe cognitive impairment lack the motor skills required to walk or eat. Usually, their agitation and anxiety increase, as do irrational fears like an aversion to water or believing they are being poisoned."

Nicole's lips were moving and sound was coming out, but I'd been unable to listen past the words "bowel" and "control." All of a sudden, *I* felt like a metronome, ticking left and right. No center. She was talking about Paul. Judge Agarra. My man. My there kind of guy.

"This may have happened anyway," she said. "Even without surgery. I understand your husband had been experiencing cognitive decline?"

"Nothing like this."

"The brain is the most complex organ in the human body. Some impairments appear suddenly, after a mini-stroke. Even with Alzheimer's disease, there is no definitive test for it while a patient is alive. Paul may have already been in an early stage. It's impossible to pinpoint an exact cause and effect."

There were those two words again. "Cause" and "effect." After Paul's surgery, I heard doctors say them often. As if no one could be blamed for what was happening. As if my husband's brain had a mind of its own. John angrily said, "They're protecting themselves from a lawsuit." It may have been true. All I knew was: Paul had been okay before. Faltering, yes. Unlike himself. Definitely. But he hadn't needed a nursing home. Before.

"Do you have long-term care insurance?" Nicole asked, softly.

"Um, no."

"Ah."

I didn't appreciate her judgy look. Opening my mouth to tell her that we'd considered it several years ago, I said, instead, "I read an article."

She said, "Oh?"

"About the downsides. You know, the truth."

With a small nod, she smiled through tight lips. I knew that she knew what I meant. You had to pay a fortune for *years* before you needed it; then, when you did need it, there was a waiting period and all manner of hoops to jump through. Especially in New York, where world-class health care has extended elderly life to the point of prolonged disability. Available nursing home beds are as hard to find as an affordable apartment, when you can find one that takes your policy at all. And, many long-term care policies cap the daily nursing home payment at one hundred dollars per day. A joke in Manhattan.

"The patient isn't doing any of the footwork, is he? The caretaker is. Am I right?" Blood jetted through my veins.

Evenly, Nicole said, "With the help of a social worker, of course."

"Ah. Good. So, since you're here, you can help me understand the waiting period, the prequalification, the 'substantial need' clause as defined by the insurance company, not the caretaker who's going out of her mind. What does 'healthy' mean, anyway? Can you qualify to even buy long-term care insurance if you have osteoporosis? Arthritis? A family history of cancer? Certainly not early Alzheimer's or a touch of dementia! Oh. Oops. We don't like to use that word."

As she had before, Nicole leaned close to me and set her cool hand on top of mine. "This certainly is a distressing time."

A laugh spurted out. "Yeah, I'd say so. Make sure

you tell your other clients to read the fine print in their policies. Like the requirement that their facility must have a nurse on duty 24/7 when many facilities have a nurse on duty for twelve hours and on *call* for the rest. I'm sure some lawyer came up with that ditty. Can you believe the scam?"

My cheeks flushed pink. "Sorry," I said, hanging my head. "Distress."

Nicole nodded and returned her features to social worker mode: slightly raised brows and a starchy smile meant to convey the ideal blend of empathy and sympathy. With forced calm, I slowly said, "Paul's father died of a heart attack at forty-eight. His brother had a heart attack in his sleep, his sister died of heart disease before her seventieth birthday. Paul and I both knew how he was going to die."

"I understand," she replied. "Many families with your resources hire an elder attorney to help them spend down to Medicaid."

Chapter Twenty-nine

The sun rose in the morning and the moon rose at night. Ordinary life rolled along. Impossible, it seemed, but it did. New Yorkers descended into the subways and climbed onto city buses. Delivery boys in floppy helmets pedaled their bikes through red lights. Nannies pushed strollers with one hand and texted with the other. Dog walkers steered their charges into the park. People got on with it. Amazing.

As if to mock the black hole our lives had been sucked into, sunlight flooded our apartment despite the nippy air outside. The turquoise sky beyond the windows was electric.

After Paul's surgery, I'd done what doctors tell people not to do: I went online. Pages of blue links popped into view. Statistical abstracts. Downward charts. Blogs. The mouse felt icy in my hand. I clicked, scrolled, read, watched, listened, and felt the weight of my sinking organs.

Postoperative cognitive dysfunction. POCD.

Why had I never heard of this?

"My wife unbuttoned her blouse in the supermarket, muttering, 'Hot, hot.' She's lost her inhibitions."

"Dad is freaking out all the time. He used to be calm."

"Can someone please explain 'executive function' to me? Mom's neuro says she's lost *it*, but I'm not clear on what *it* was."

"Help! My husband bursts into rages for no reason. What can I do?"

Nothing. That was the horrible answer. Nothing could be done.

Anesthesiologist associations denied the sedation connection. No way to determine cause and effect. *Anecdotal* evidence. Yet, practicing anesthesiologists wrote journal articles advising colleagues to alert their patients to a problem that seemed to be growing by the day. Researchers wanted more studies on POCD. But how could they conduct them? Who would volunteer to go under the knife to see if their brain was ruined when they woke up? How could a physician assemble a control group? Instead, doctors—and social workers—noted the postsurgical deficits reported by families: loss of short-term memory and focus, inability to manage time, problems talking, lower inhibitions, higher anxiety, personality changes. Loss of executive function: the mental skills that help you get things done.

Over and over, I read versions of the same theme: "After the surgery, my elderly husband—wife, mother, father, grandmother, grandfather, aunt, uncle, sister, brother—was never the same." When the patient lived at all. Mortality rates took my breath away.

In the loneliness of my apartment—how had I ever longed for such silence?—guilt devoured me. Had I known, I would have told the doctors, "Paul hasn't been himself." I would have made them listen to me. Though, what could they do? *Un*break his shoulder? Operate without anesthesia?

Nothing could be done. POCD was a heartbreaking waiting game.

I'd turned the computer off and went to bed alone.

While I slept that night, I dreamed I woke up. I was in our apartment. It was a morning like any other morning. My eyes fluttered open at first light. I stretched both elbows out and rolled my neck. In my dream, I suddenly froze. The silence in our bedroom unnerved me. No snoring from the other side of the bed. No guttural plaints of Paul's nightmares. Lola was sitting on the rug, staring at me. She already knew. One look in her eyes and I knew, too. My heart dropped like a stone in a still lake. I burrowed my face into the pillow and tried to fall back asleep. Childlike, I pretended that a monster wasn't under the bed. *In* bed with me. I pled for unconsciousness to erase what I knew to be true.

"Ten more minutes," I begged God. Let the last drip of my old life run dry before the new one crushed me.

But, of course, sleep was impossible.

Biting down on my molars, I steeled myself. Gently peeling back the covers, I swung my legs onto the floor. I placed my warm hand on Lola's head. "Stay close to me," I whispered, even as I knew she would. For once.

Still too frightened to turn around, I dreamed that I walked to the window and slid the bedroom curtains all the way open. I smoothed them into pools of fabric on either side of the sill. Gazing into the world beyond our apartment, I assessed the day, knowing it would be one I'd relive over and over.

"It was the most beautiful sunny morning."

"It rained so hard the sky was weeping."

"My heart broke when I saw the fresh dusting of snow. Paul loved this time of year."

Barefoot, feeling the cool roughness of our wood floor, I tiptoed to Paul's side of the bed. My hand pressed hard on my chest to keep my heart from splitting in two. First, I saw a lump of bedding. My love's outline.

Next, I saw him. In peaceful stillness, with both hands curled on top of the covers, my husband was where he always was in the early morning. Only now, he wasn't there at all. His mouth was open, his eyes halfway shut. For a moment I marveled at the obviousness of death It was so far from sleeping, so clearly lifeless.

As an iceberg calving, I suddenly felt the violence of separation. The abrupt oneness of my new life. Never again would the world look the same. Sunsets would feel unbearably sad; birthday cakes would reduce me to tears. My ring finger would be naked. My hand wouldn't look like my hand at all. I'd be a widow, no longer a wife. A woman who belonged to no one. No longer could I sign e-mails, "Love, us." My "us" was gone for good. The gutting of that thought turned my legs to jelly. In my nightmare, I stumbled into the easy chair beside our bed and liquefied. Wailing for Paul. For me. For all we would never again be.

I woke up on a wet pillow.

Before anyone could stop me, I dressed and fed Lola and took the crosstown bus to the hospital to sign Paul's release papers. I left Nicole's "Agarra" file at the apartment, on top of the recycling bin. No way was I putting my husband in a nursing home. He was coming home with me. Where he belonged.

Chapter Thirty

On most days, our block is pretty. Even on wintry days. The street is wide. There are stoops in front of the brownstones on one side, doormen in front of the prewars on the other. Real estate listings call it "tree-lined" even when the trees are bare. That day—the day I brought Paul home—was especially stunning. Garbage had been picked up that morning; supers had hosed down the sidewalks before shutting off their water. First snow was on its way. The air was sharp and clear.

"What the hell is that for?" Paul had sneered at the metal cane the hospital had provided. He threw it in the back of the cab I'd hailed for us at the hospital. Like a crotchety old man in a smelly cardigan, he inched forward, grousing beneath his breath. He refused the support of my arm. Instead, Paul took so long getting himself situated in the backseat, the driver started the meter.

Paul's language skills had returned. Despite the swearing and grumbling, I'd seen it as a hopeful sign. But I knew nothing back then.

That first day, as we turned the corner onto our block, a grin widened my husband's face. Sunlight reflected off the wet sidewalks. Dogs trotted to the park ahead of their walkers, at the taut end of their leashes. Top dogs all. When the cab pulled up to our front door, Paul gazed at our building with the wonder of a child. It had been a week since the ambulance had sirened him away. Astonishing to think of it, really. I felt aged, as if I'd missed my last birthday. Or two. Yet Paul's abrupt boyishness lifted my spirits. He squeezed my hand and said, "Home."

Yes. Home.

My husband accepted my help getting out of the cab. I paid the driver, then ran around to open Paul's door. Gripping his good arm, I rocked him back and forth to work up the momentum to pull his body up. Once he was upright, the driver chirped, "Well done!" That cracked us both up.

"What happened, Judge?" The doorman across the street saw Paul's shoulder sling and called out to us.

"Broken shoulder," I yelled back. We'd known that

doorman for years. He guarded the elegant entrance to the prewar opposite our front door. All day, every day, he watched *our* comings and goings. "The only brownstone in Manhattan with a full-service doorman," Paul often quipped. Then he'd tilt his head back and release the laugh that I loved.

Making a face, the doorman yelped, "Yeowcha."

Paul shouted to him, "You look fat."

I froze. My eyes sprung open. "Painkillers!" Flapping my hand in a quick goodbye, I maneuvered Paul inside. Is that what they meant by a loss of inhibitions? Was my man going to unzip his pants in the supermarket?

"Lola can't wait to see you." I changed the subject.

"John's daughter?"

From the start, I saw what I was in for.

Incredibly, Lola didn't bark when the key unlocked our downstairs door. The moment she saw Paul, she leaped up and ran to him. Our recalcitrant dog wagged her whole body. She cried, whimpered, and moaned with delight at the sight and smell of her master.

"Lulu!" he gushed. "My girl."

Our Lola didn't care that Paul got her name wrong. She leaned into his legs and stretched her muzzle up to his face. She gazed into his eyes with pure adoration. Before she could knock him over, I sat Paul on the bench in front of our bed. He ran his hand over Lola's furry forehead and down her silky ears. He cooed, "It's okay, it's okay." Paul seemed to understand that his dog needed to be forgiven for hurting him. He stroked her back and tickled the top of her freckled head. Rapturously, he said, "Our cat has finally become a dog."

The most normal thing he'd said all day.

Stairs. Area rugs. Throw rugs. A bathmat. Uneven backyard brick. Lola underfoot. Our apartment was full of tripping hazards.

"'The brain is disremembering the motor skills of walking,'" I read online. "'Instead, the feet shuffle.'"

"Disremembering." I liked that word. It sounded less permanent than cognitive impairment or dementia or the awful *A* word. If you disremembered something, you could *disforget* it, too. Right?

While Paul napped, I got busy. I tightly rolled rugs and tied them with twine. I dragged them downstairs to our basement storage space. I draped our bathmat on a towel rack. Off the floor, within reach. I called my brother in California.

"I need you," I said.

"On my way," he replied, as I knew he would.

———

Nathan Thayer was saddled with a lispy birth name, too. Only it didn't bother him. Some people called him "Nate," but most didn't. Like Paul, my brother was a *there* kind of guy. A professional cabinetmaker, he could build anything. He still lived in our childhood home. Only he'd made it his own. Custom cabinetry in every room. White walls, dark wood floors. Simple and uncluttered. Like his single, childless life. Sort of. Even though his divorce was years ago, my brother still wore his ring.

"Can't get it off," he claimed. Nathan's broken heart, I knew, had once been filled to capacity.

When I called my brother, I told him what I'd already ordered online: knob covers for our gas stove, safety drawer latches and cabinet catches, motion-activated night-lights, an anti-scalding attachment for the tub faucet.

"Babyproofing for a giant baby?" he asked.

"Exactly." We both found that hilarious. Which felt as luscious as hot chocolate on an icy afternoon. My brother and I understood that laughter is a strong branch to grab when life falls off a cliff and you're clawing at twigs on the way down.

John found nothing funny at all.

"Dad!" From the start, he shouted in his father's

face whenever he flew in from Boston. "Another CFO was indicted. Finally, they're cracking down on false financial statements." Sitting beside Paul, John flipped through the *Times*'s business section, page by page. As many people did in the first few months, he mistook his father's blank expressions for an inability to hear. He believed he could restore Paul's cognition by yelling current events at him. "Let's see what's up in IPO news."

"Dirty bastards," Paul would blurt out, making me and Nathan laugh.

John didn't laugh at anything. "You remember the election, don't you, Dad? Let's see what's happening in Washington."

When Kate joined her husband, she bustled into the apartment with groceries from Whole Foods. Blueberries, walnuts, avocados, wild salmon. "Can't have too much brain food!" she trilled, as if I fed Paul a diet of Doritos. Brenda showed up with bundles of gotu kola from her garden.

"It's Ayurvedic," she proudly stated, as if I knew what that meant.

At the beginning, friends and colleagues from the courthouse dropped by with dumplings from Paul's favorite lunch spot in Chinatown, and gift baskets from Zabar's. "Paul isn't off gluten, is he?"

It didn't take long to hear excuses for not visiting more often. I understood. It was painful to watch a brilliant mind fade before your eyes. Still, our best friends, like Anita and Isaac, settled in for the long haul.

"What's on the calendar this month?" Paul's face lit up whenever Isaac came over.

"Court is in recess, Judge," Isaac lied.

"Ah. How's the baby?"

"Trey? He'll be four soon."

"Ah. What's on the calendar this month?"

"Court is in recess, Judge."

Eventually, Isaac helped me file Paul's pension paperwork. Surprising us all—even the neurologist, a new doctor added to the list—Judge Agarra showed no desire to get back on the bench. Aside from his circular conversations with Isaac, the profession Paul once adored was both out of his sight and out of his mind.

By far, Paul's favorite visitor—and mine—was Edie. Whenever she followed her parents or her grandmother through the door, Paul beamed. When he no longer had words, he slapped his hand over his heart. He thumped his cane on the floor. He never yelped in pain around her, as he did when the physical therapist made him work his shoulder or use his thigh muscles to lift his feet.

"Let's see the Hudson, Granddad."

At every level of Paul's decline, Edie did what she always did with her grandfather: walk to Riverside Park to watch the Hudson River flow. When Paul got worse, they moved more slowly. With infinite patience, she helped him insert his socked feet into the Velcro sneakers I'd bought him online. She ran a comb through his wispy hair and leashed Lola so she could walk with them, too. If Paul got tired in the park, they sat on a bench with Lola nestled at their feet. After he lost the ability to walk at all, Edie strapped Lola to Paul's wheelchair and strolled the three of them along the promenade and past the crab apple grove, delighting in the way the tiny whitecaps danced across the gray ribbon of the river.

"Dad isn't getting better." At home in Boston, John Agarra moaned to his wife. Edie didn't want to hear it.

"Why not appreciate everything Granddad can do, instead of stressing over what he can't?"

Our teenage sage educated us all.

Chapter Thirty-one

As days do, they became weeks and months. Long ago, I finished painting the lampshades I had on order. Initially, I temporarily suspended my Etsy site. Then I canceled it altogether. Paul was my job now. I made him fish tacos and rigatoni with garlic and oil. I helped my creative genius of a brother retrofit our apartment.

Nathan bought a length of bronze pipe—matching our bathroom fixtures—and installed it in the wall-to-wall enclosure around our bathtub. He made a grab bar that looked like a ballet barre. Using the same sturdy pipe, he fashioned railings on either side of the toilet that somehow looked like a cool art installation instead of the means to help Paul's wobbly legs lift him up. Remembering how much I'd hated living in our "sick house"—Mom's amber pill vials the centerpiece on our kitchen table—Nathan used his cabinetry skills to build a lockable bedside table with a pullout shelf for pills, dispensers for baby wipes and tissues, and a caddy for a water pitcher and cup. To enclose the staircase, both upstairs and down, he built gates that resembled entrances to a country garden. He painted the white pickets matte because he'd read that glare upset people in later stages of cognitive decline.

My amazing brother made our new life feel alive.

"Why are you doing this?" Paul asked him.

Nathan replied, "Getting ready for whatever may come."

Dressed in his work jeans, ready to help, Paul initially said, "If you need a hand, I'm here. Strong shoulder? Not so much."

In those early days, my husband's humor popped up like a jack-in-the-box. Delighting us each time. As suddenly, his former self disappeared.

"Why are you doing this?" Paul asked Nathan, over and over.

"Getting ready for whatever may come."

My brother showed me what love looks like.

Little by little, Paul left me. After his surgery, my husband was never the same. The trajectory of his decline resembled the stock market chart from the seventies.

Brief pops of hope. Ultimately, though, I learned to join Paul in his reality, instead of wishing, praying, begging God, pestering the neurologist, feeding him blueberries and oily fish and herbs from Brenda's garden in the hopes that he would return to mine.

Some days were calm. Almost normal. Other days, I felt like I was living in the middle of an icy lake. Cracks everywhere. Frozen in panic. At any moment, I could be plunged into its frigid depths.

When the frustration of losing words made Paul shout at me, I retreated to the bathroom and whispered "let" on the inhale and "go" on the exhale. If that didn't work, I popped a Xanax. When my frustration made me shout at him, I called Anita and wept. She knew better than to tell me everything was going to be okay.

On the worst days, when I missed the man I married so acutely it felt like my heart was already broken beyond repair, I left him with his health aide and took Lola on a special walk. Away from the sad faces of our neighbors: "How is he doing? How are you holding up?" Together, Lola and I disappeared into the green wonderland of Hudson Crescent. So I could hide. So I could cry behind my sunglasses.

Chapter Thirty-two

August in New York is a punishment. The humidity is so oppressive I often wake up with a headache and go to sleep with a migraine. Tylenol is useless. Sumatriptan only softens the throbbing in my head. Temporary relief comes solely after a cool shower or a large bowl of ice cream. In summer, I live for brain freeze.

Lola loved the heat. A reminder of her steamy origins, apparently. Like clockwork, she padded over to me at eight in the morning and eight in the evening. Her two walk times. If I didn't jump up and grab her leash, or get her ready for the nighttime dog walker— a necessary indulgence—she drilled her stink eyes into me until I did my duty. So she could do hers.

"Okay, okay," I said, at five past eight one hot August morning. "Hold your horses."

Paul was asleep. Amoy was upstairs. It was her early shift. I heard her footsteps overhead, smelled her fried johnnycakes.

"Should Paul be eating so much grease?" Last time she visited, Kate Agarra had watched Paul's health aide cook her Jamaican specialties. Cornering me downstairs, her button nose wrinkled in distaste, she said, "They're, like, *dripping.*"

"He likes it," I'd said, shrugging my shoulders.

"Where's the lean protein? Omega-threes?"

I didn't have the heart to say, "What's the point?" Paul rarely remembered to eat anything anymore.

Anita—my incredible friend—found Amoy for us. She took Ubers to the home health aide training schools around New York. She arrived at lunchtime with cookies from Make My Cake bakery in Harlem.

"Anyone peckish?"

Who could resist a freshly baked chocolate chip cookie? While the students snacked, Anita asked questions.

"Where are you from?"

"What is your family like?"

"Can you lift one hundred and eighty pounds?"

Agency recruiters were there, too. They had their own snacks on offer. All gave Anita their business cards. But, Anita figured, why not give the salary directly to the aide herself?

Of course, I thought I could manage alone. And I could. For a while. Paul could be left alone back then. He didn't have panic attacks or fly into rages for no reason. Back then. We lived in a loving cocoon. Our little family ate meals together and watched movies on TV. We ambled through the park and took the bus to Whole Foods. We ordered in and sat in our backyard sipping wine. We took siestas. When John and Kate flew in from Boston, we went out to dinner in the neighborhood. When Edie was with them, I cooked dinner so we could all feel normal.

We had settled into our new normal. Until the unsettling day when everything changed.

It was early. On a Sunday. The front door buzzed and Lola went berserk. Stupidly, we thought age would mellow her out. Mother Nature had other ideas. Still in bed, I rolled over and groaned. Paul wasn't there. He was already up. "Is that Brenda?" I shouted upstairs. Who else would it be?

Bzzzz. Bzzzz. Bark. Bark.

"Paul!" He didn't answer. Lately, he'd been listening to CDs nonstop. The old blues songs he loved. His ears were always covered in giant blue headphones.

Normally a good thing. Music kept him calm. That morning, though, I was annoyed. Would Brenda ever leave us alone?

Angrily flipping the covers back, I stood up and slapped my bare feet to the door. "What?" I said into the intercom, my irritation obvious.

"NYPD."

My heart lurched. Still in my pajamas, I flung open the door and felt the blood drain from my face. Through the window in our exterior door, I saw two police officers. Paul stood, befuddled, between them. I ran down the hall and opened the door.

"Does this man live here?" one of the officers asked me.

"Yes! He's my husband. What happened?"

"We found him at the church on West End. He was trying to unlock their side door. This address was in his wallet."

"Paul?" His face was blank. I'd seen that *non*look before.

"Do you need us to call social services?" the officer asked.

"No. Of course not. Thank you for bringing him home."

The officer said, "If he's found wandering without ID, he'll be taken to the emergency room."

There it was. The word that every caretaker dreaded most: "wandering."

With a nod, I thanked the officers profusely. Then I gently led my husband inside, down the hall, to our home. He wore slippers and his Patagonia parka. Shuffling, he mumbled, "Closing arguments." Then he melted into me and began to cry.

So Anita found Amoy for us.

"It means 'beautiful goddess' in Jamaican," she told me, beaming. The name suited Paul's aide perfectly. Closely cropped hair, long limbs, arm definition to rival a long-distance runner's. Her full lips were pink; her skin was as smooth as satin. "Paul will love her," Anita said.

She was right, of course. The first thing Amoy said to Paul was, "I don't want any trouble from *you*." We all laughed. Especially Paul. Amoy got us from the start. The last thing Paul—or I—wanted was for him to be treated like an invalid. Lola loved her, too.

"Miss Boonoonoonoos," Amoy cooed at her. It was Jamaican slang for "sweetie." Lola was a wriggling puppy around her. Our cat had become a dog for good. Or maybe it was the pieces of jerked chicken Amoy snuck her. More than once, I'd smelled allspice on Lola's breath.

Shortly after eight, one hot August morning, I pulled

on shorts and a T-shirt, strapped Lola into her harness, and headed for Hudson Crescent. "See you in a bit," I quietly called up to Amoy. Standing at the top of the stairs, she called down to Lola, "No raccoons for you."

Off we went.

It was the sort of day that produced visible heat waves. We ran across the hot asphalt street and made our way to the dappled shade surrounding 1118 and your beautiful granite steps. Months had passed since I'd last seen the pediatrician in the patch of green across from your sparkling glass door. So much had happened, I rarely thought about him anymore. He'd almost certainly moved away. Perhaps he'd retired to his upstate organic farm? I didn't dare imagine the worst: that he'd been killed by sniper fire in Afghanistan. Or he'd contracted dengue fever while caring for homeless children in Sri Lanka. All I knew was that I was proud of him. Rare was the selfless soul who would forgo the comfort of a spacious two-bedroom, two-bath, high-ceilinged apartment with old world detailing, a Thermador oven in an eat-in kitchen, and breathtaking wraparound views. Or so I imagined. It was possible he lived in a large one-bedroom with a compact washer/dryer tucked into the walk-in closet. He probably donated half his salary to charity, anyway.

"Heel." Just before your glossy front door, Lola

intensely sniffed the rail around your tree and flower bed. A moment longer and she would squirt. I knew the signs. Not that I would let that happen to your summer begonias.

"Hey there, Spot."

A male voice tumbled down from your front steps. Lola, I swear, looked up and rolled her eyes. She hated to be called "Spot." Or worse: "Freckle Face."

I turned my head and lost my breath. There he was. Blake. The pediatrician. Back from the front lines. My cheeks flushed bright pink.

"Dalmatian?" he asked, walking toward us.

I giggled like a girl. "A common misconception."

Lifting her leg like a boy, Lola peed on the flowers. I stared crazily into the pediatrician's eyes hoping he wouldn't notice.

"She's a Catahoula mix."

"Cata*huh*?"

Overlaughing, "Oh, hee, hee, ha, ha, *ha*," I chirped, "Exactly. I'd never heard of one, either. She's a rescue from the South."

My voice, I noticed, mimicked the squeal of a guinea pig.

Blake bent down to pat Lola's head. It was clear he didn't know dogs. He bounced his hand on her head like it was a basketball.

"I'm Fay," I blurted out, holding out my hand before Lola bit his.

"Jim." He straightened, smiled, and shook my hand.

"Jim? Is that some sort of nickname?"

"I guess so. I was born a James."

James? I was confused. *Was James a nickname for Blake?*

"I love your building," I confessed, carefully withholding the depth of my desire and hoping he wouldn't judge the sad state of my outfit. I didn't want to seem like an apartment stalker. Jim quickly replied, "I've lived here a long time."

"Ah."

As every New Yorker knows, that's code for "I bought when it was cheap." Which showed how savvy my man was. It could also mean his apartment was rent regulated. Which I hoped *not*. Rent regulation was the city's dirty little secret. Study after study had found that artificially lowering market rents for some only raised the rents on everyone else. Instead of making the city more affordable to the masses, the lucky few with a rent-regulated deal—nearly all with secret summer homes in the Hamptons or on the Jersey shore—made it impossible for newcomers to live in the city without a roommate (or two) and a bedroom window that opened onto an air shaft. Yet another way the rich got richer.

Still, it was the city's political third rail. Protesters with sweet apartment deals were loud and organized. They couldn't care less about anyone else.

No way was my selfless Jim Blake one of *those*.

"I live in a brownstone," I said. "A doorman is a distant dream."

Lola pulled me toward the park. I raised my hand to wave goodbye and curved my lips into a seductive smile. Shocking me in a thrilling sort of way, Jim moved with us. In a quick swipe, I ran my tongue over my teeth to make sure I'd remembered to brush. I had. Thank you, *God*.

Hearing only the clicking of Lola's toenails on the sidewalk and the thumping of my heart, I ransacked my brain for something pithy to say. I felt like I knew him. We'd been through so much together. Yet tumbleweeds blew through my brain. In my peripheral vision, I was startled to see that the pediatrician wore orange shorts and white socks with brown sandals. His short-sleeved shirt was as wrinkled as a shar-pei. Was he on his way to the hardware store? Repainting his apartment on such a hot day? Didn't physicians have people do such things? Surely Juan Carlos, his doorman, could suggest someone. Also, when Jim had gripped my hand to shake it, I couldn't help but notice the dark line beneath his—longish—fingernails. Had he been organic gardening at dawn that morning on his upstate farm? Maybe volunteer weeding in Riverside Park?

"I can only imagine how hot it is in Africa," I said, finally, glancing at Jim with compassion. "Or the southern tip of Asia. That's where Sri Lanka is, right? Global warming must be torture there."

"*Pfft*. That hoax."

"What hoax?"

"Historically, the earth *always* gets hotter or colder. It's nature, not anything man-made. Nature will fix herself. That's what she does."

My lower lip flapped open. "How can a scientist say that?" I stared at the pediatrician, agog.

"Exactly. How can a scientist say that? How does he know?"

Jim began a rant. "Fake news media will print or say anything. Our country is full of sheep. They'll believe whatever they are spoon-fed."

Tempted to remind him that I'd seen him reading the *New York Post*, a newspaper that regularly reported UFO sightings, I stopped myself. I didn't want to sound too, well, sheepish. Like I only read the *New York Times* because every smart person I knew did.

"At my shop—"

"Shop?" I asked. Did pediatricians have a storefront?

"Locked and Loaded. On Broadway."

I lurched to a halt right there on the sidewalk.

"You're a . . . *locksmith*?"

Admittedly, it came out snootier than I'd intended. There's nothing wrong with the honest work of a locksmith. In fact, one had saved my rear end last month when my key broke off in our downstairs door and Paul was having a meltdown. But Locked and Loaded? I'd walked past that sliver of a shop many times, too scared to go in because it sounded like they secretly sold guns under the counter. Or that the locksmith would have beer on his breath at ten in the morning.

"My father started the business years ago," Jim said. "He left it to me."

"So you repair locks as, um, a hobby?"

He laughed.

"Like, when you're not at the hospital?" I ventured. "Or in the Middle East?"

"Middle East? Who would go to that hellhole?"

My head was spinning. I looked at Jim and suddenly noticed that his glasses weren't tortoiseshell at all. They were brown plastic.

Jim flicked his head back toward you—the stately building that still made me burn with desire. "Only in

America, am I right?" he chuckled. "A guy like me can live in a building like that. And get this: My apartment is rent controlled. Not stabilized. *Controlled.* Beautiful!"

No kidding, I heard my upper lashes hitting my lower lids. I looked up to see if I could spot a hidden camera.

"I played it smart," Jim went on. "The minute my mother got sick, I changed my mailing address to hers. Got rid of my landline, all that. You have to prove you live there, you know? Not that I did, of course. But, after she passed—God rest her soul—I sneaked my stuff in little by little in the service elevator. Now, they can't get me out. Ha! Guess what I pay in rent? You won't believe it. Guess."

A wave of nausea gripped my stomach. "I'd rather not," I said.

Together, we crossed Riverside Drive into the park. My forehead felt sweaty. I'd forgotten my sun hat. I began to wonder if Jim was going to tag along the whole way.

"Whoa, girl," I said to Lola, extending my arm as if she were tugging at the leash. For once, she wasn't. Her entire head was poked into a hedge. The leash looked like a limp jump rope.

"Here's a hint," said Jim. "I pay more each month

for a two-hundred-square-foot shop than I do for my two-bedroom with one and a half baths."

A dry heave constricted my airway.

"Interesting," I croaked, hoping he would peel off.

He didn't.

By the time we reached the crab apple grove, and the dirt path next to it, I was plotting ways to escape. Jim blabbered nonstop. He did live on a high floor—though not the penthouse, he told me with his lower lip protruded as if he'd been robbed—and he did have a wraparound river view.

"Of course, my landlord hates me. He pays triple in maintenance what I pay in rent. And it's locked in for life. Sweet! All the co-op owners in the building hate me, too." He laughed meanly. Ha. *Ha*. "The co-op gets a hefty flip tax if I move out and the owner sells. Not that I would ever move out. Unless I decide to live full-time at my summerhouse in Montauk."

"Nice meeting you."

Abruptly, I stopped and extended my hand. Though I didn't want to touch Jim again. I stood inches from his face. How had I never noticed how permy his hair looked? His horse teeth were the color of old mac and cheese. He made Paul look like a college student. Where was Blake's selflessness? His air of kindness? I waited for Jim to take my hand so I could pump it once and let go of it—and my fantasy—forever. Stunning me, Jim grabbed my palm and pulled it toward his body like he was catching a line drive. He held on, even when I tugged a little.

"See you around the neighborhood," he said. Only, it was more of a question. *See you around the neighborhood?* As if he hoped we'd meet and walk and chat again.

"Oh. Well. You know." I smiled with my lips alone. "Lola, *come.*" She had plopped down in the dirt and was chewing on a stick as if it were a porky Slim Jim. When I pulled on the leash, she rolled over and went limp. I was familiar with her passive resistance. She often used it when she didn't want to go home at the end of her walk. Nonetheless, I dragged her sixty-pound body sideways through the dust. Stubborn mule.

Out of nowhere, a squirrel darted across the path. Its tail flicked like a question mark on a hot grill. Instantly on her feet, Lola lunged for it, nearly popping my shoulder out of its socket. Some things never change. I yelped in pain. But it was worth it. Off we flew.

"Bye, Freckle Face!" Jim called after us.

As a final goodbye, I flapped my hand in the air behind my head. Then I wiped it on my shorts.

Even after the squirrel was up a tree, mocking us, we

ran. Sweat dribbled down my temples; Lola's tongue hung sideways out of her mouth. Still, we kept up the pace until Jim was out of view and the pediatrician was out of my head—and heart—forever. Slowing at last, I gulped the warm, wet air. I gasped, "Good girl." Lola raised her heavy eyelids. It may have been my imagination, but I think I saw her twitch her head as if to say, "Don't worry, Mom. I've got your back."

We continued our walk the way we did every day. Lola in the lead. Top dog. At the end of the promenade, beneath the shade of a mature elm, we sat on a bench and soaked in the beauty of our park. Like a poet, Lola sighed and gazed at the glistening Hudson River. I grinned. Then, I bent down to kiss my beautiful headstrong dog on the tip of her lovely speckled nose. With a lap of her skinny pink tongue, Lola kissed me back.

Chapter Thirty-three

My eyes fluttered open at first light. As they always did, whether I slept well or not. I stretched both elbows out, rolled my neck. Lola sat on the floor beside the bed, staring at me. I reached down to run my thumb up and down the space between her eyebrows—my favorite spot—then stopped. The silence was alarming. No whooshing of Paul's CPAP. No snoring from the sleep apnea that had finally been diagnosed and treated. My heart dropped like a stone in a still lake. A flash of fear engulfed me. I pressed my eyes shut. But, of course, sleep was impossible.

Biting down on my molars, I steeled myself. I swallowed my rising panic. Gently peeling back the covers, I swung my legs onto the floor. I rested my warm palm on Lola's head.

"Stay close to me," I whispered. For once, she obeyed.

Too frightened to turn around, I walked to the window and slid the bedroom curtains all the way open. I smoothed them into pools of fabric on either side of the sill. It was the most beautiful fall morning. The birch leaves in our backyard trees were the color of pumpkin flesh; sunlight filtered through them in flickering diagonal lines. My heart broke. Paul loved this time of year. Almost as much as the dusting of first snow.

Barefoot, feeling the cool roughness of our wood floor, I tiptoed around our bed to Paul's side. Lola's toenails *click, clicked* beside me. She leaned against my leg. Inch by inch, we approached. With my hand pressed on my chest to keep my heart from busting apart, I looked up. First, I saw a lump of bedding. It was the body pillow I'd placed along the edge of the bed to keep Paul from falling off. Lola and I crept forward, onto the large memory-foam mat I put on the wood floor at night in case he fell anyway. My husband often thrashed in his sleep.

In the gauzy light, I saw my love's outline. Then I saw him. In peaceful stillness, with both hands on top of the covers, Paul was where he always was when a new day began.

"*Mmkaw.*" A guttural sound lanced the silence. Then the snorting gasp I knew so well. Paul's snoring revved up like a lawn mower.

At my feet, Lola rotated in a tight circle. She dropped heavily onto the soft mat. Contentedly, she sighed. One of my favorite sounds in the world. That and the sound of Paul breathing.

"My love." Gently, I brushed back the wisps of hair on my husband's forehead. I inhaled his Paul smell. His CPAP, I noticed, had been thrown to the floor. Careful not to wake him—though I did—I removed the body pillow along the edge and climbed into bed with him. I tucked myself under the covers next to my man. When he opened his eyes, I whispered, "It's okay. It's me." He stared blindly at the ceiling. One hand reached up to pat his face. He knew something was missing.

"Your CPAP is off. It's okay."

Taking my husband's hand in mine, I intertwined our fingers. With my thumb, I massaged circles in his palm. He loved that. It calmed him. I stretched my neck to kiss the soft spot beneath his chin. The spot that I owned. Quietly, I said, "Go back to sleep, my sweet. Day is still on its way."

Paul opened his mouth, then closed it again. He no longer had words. Almost everything he'd once been was gone. He was now frail, skinny, silent. Paul was never hungry anymore, but he was often thirsty. The water pitcher on the nightstand that Nathan built had been replaced with a giant sippy cup full of fruit juice.

"Sugar is so toxic," Kate whined to me. To Paul, she said, "Here, Dad, try this coconut water."

More than once, Paul had thrown the contents of his sippy cup in his daughter-in-law's face. "Don't take it personally," I told her, even as I glanced at Paul and sometimes noted a twinkle in his eyes.

From time to time, Paul's eyes would flash white. They would dart wildly around the room. A hallucination, I knew. Sometimes frightening, sometimes not. Once, when he still had words, he told me that he saw his father sitting at the family's piano. Cigarette dangling between his lips, its ash curved and ready to fall, he played and winked at his son. Paul had laughed like a boy. Enchantment brought color to his cheeks.

Other times, his hands would flail. He'd rip at the covers, my hair, his crotch. I learned how to interpret his body language. Amoy taught me how to step into Paul's reality. "When he's frustrated, join him there," she said. "Tell him, 'It must feel awful right now.' When he's scared, reassure him he's safe with you. The monsters will go away."

Month after month, I did just that. Even as my fear

of losing him was always the beast lurking beneath my side of the bed.

With my husband's hand in mine, I stroked the flesh between his knuckles and the ropy tendons that ran down to his bony wrist. I kissed each fingertip: *pop, pop, pop.* The rise and fall of his chest was as soothing as the ebb and flow of the ocean. Like Lola, I sighed contentedly.

Suddenly, Paul opened his eyes. When I looked into their gingerbread depths, I saw him. My man. My there kind of guy. Sucking in air, I gasped, "My love, have you come back to me?"

He smiled and squeezed my hand. Words weren't needed for me to understand: *I never left.*

Acknowledgments

To my amazing agent, Laura Langlie: Thank you, my friend, for always being there when I need you, and when I don't yet realize I need you. You're the best.

To the editor of my dreams, Carrie Feron: Without you, I never would have seen the forest for the trees. Again, you saved me from myself. Gratitude is an inadequate word.

Heartfelt thanks to: Etta Phifer for her friendship and generosity, the extraordinary women at Dorot in New York City for their unwavering support, and Valentina Harrell for her ear, her brain, and her heart.

To the loyal friends I've neglected while burrowed into this book—Linda, Su, Rosemarie, Kathy, Karen, Carol, Tony, Joanna, Bill, and others—your understanding and patience mean everything to me.

A whopping "Wahoo!" to everyone at William Morrow, especially marketing director Molly Waxman, who is as nice as she is smart; Carolyn Coons, who is always gracious and helpful; and an art department that never fails to design book covers I am gaga over. Lucky me to have a great publisher like you.

To my creative genius brother, Chris Barbera, and his awe-inspiring wife, Jill: My love is deeper than the ocean and wider than the sky.

Finally, my Bob, my love, my there kind of guy. You floor me with your resilience and ceaseless love. I am yours—in sickness and in health—for as long as we both shall live.